T010566-4

Being Menehune

My Journal

J. Arthur Rath III

iUniverse, Inc.
Bloomington

Being Menehune
My Journal

*This is a work of fiction. All of the characters, names, incidents,
organizations, and dialogue in this novel are either the products
of the author's imagination or are used fictitiously.*

iUniverse books may be ordered through booksellers or by contacting:

*iUniverse
1663 Liberty Drive
Bloomington, IN 47403
www.iuniverse.com
1-800-Authors (1-800-288-4677)*

ISBN: 978-1-4620-1892-5 (sc)
ISBN: 978-1-4620-1893-2 (ebk)

Printed in the United States of America

iUniverse rev. date: 05/19/2011

Front and back cover artwork and pages 49, 51, and 113 by Paul Forney.

Front cover art: Kupuna chanting "The Menehune Opera," on page 100.

Back cover art: Kahu, menehune mentor, and Miki, a Leprechaun, knowledgeable of fairy worlds.

For more information about this book, menehune, and fairy lore, see the two websites: *beingmenehunes.com and hawaiianfairies.com*

Dedication

"Being Menehune" is respectfully dedicated to Japan's 2011 Tsunami victims.

Hawaii's King Kalakaua invited Japan's emperor to be associated with The Kingdom of Hawaii. As this book explains, he suggested both nations' royal families be joined through marriage and that Hawai'i and Japan work together.

In recent times, Japan has became the home of Hawai'i's valued spiritual brothers and sisters. We are partners across the sea. Island *ohana* (real and extended family) are saddened by Japan's devastation and trauma.

Creativity lifts and encourages human spirit. "Aloha" from Hawaii for Japan's quick and imaginative recovery.

J. Arthur Rath III

Contents

Introduction

1. Plain Warfare. 1

2. Meeting Menehune. 12

3. Into Unseen Hawai'i 23

4. Leprechaun Miki. 27

5. How Japan Will Win. 31

6. Alienation 36

7. Japan's Hawai'i Kingdom 39

8. Going Underground 45

9. Persian Storyteller 50

10. Disguised Warrior 63

11. Battle of Chicanery 70

12. Kuali'i Visits America 76

13. Purim Party. 82

14. Kaua'i Menehune Valley 88

15. Where Time's Timeless 108

16. Mind Gardening. 123

17. Entering Oz 129

18. La-La L.A.. 137

19. Ghost House. 144

20. Bookishly Brave. 159

21. War Tremors 164

22. A Place for Us 175

23. I Discover Me 180

24. Hip-Hip Hooray, USA!. 184

25. Ancient Hawaiian Life. 192

26. Feudalism 204

27. Taxes and Games. 210

28. Money Grows on Trees 227

29. Stone Age Blasted Away. 240

30. Queen Esther's Revenge. 247

Introduction

"**Y**our author wrote every day," said the Kona, Hawai'i, librarian as I returned *A Connecticut Yankee in King Arthur's Court.*

"I read that in *The Mark Twain Journal,* a periodical. We've most of his books."

"What's a journal?"

"Similar to a diary: describing events, relating stories, explaining things."

A journal? What a neat way to retain information!

Right then, being ten in 1942, I decided to write a journal, beginning with the 1731 battle I'd just seen. Then I explained being with menehune.

I use the present tense to describe things just after they've happened, past tense for earlier occurrences.

1. Plain Warfare

Our hilltop perch makes the warriors below appear two and a half inches tall—my lead soldiers' size. Fighting will resemble pageantry from this panoramic vantage point.

I enjoy organizing tiny soldiers into battle formations as Hawaiian armies down there are doing.

Kahu, my menehune mentor, explains: "We'll see an old-style battle—"

Miki interrupts from behind us, saying, in his pseudo-Shakespearian way:

> 'Tis the Stone Age when weaponry falls short,
> Hand-to-hand killing is this form of sport,
> Body meets body with little breadth,
> Loss means slavery or an altar death.
> Sticks and stones enemy bones be breaking,
> Long sticks do spearing, short ones the stabbing.
> Rocks stun the opponents while they're running,
> Shark-teeth clubs lacerate, disemboweling.

Glancing back, I see Miki raising his eyebrows to inquire if I enjoyed his gory description. I return a blank stare. He's eliminated associations I might have had of pomp and grandeur.

Kahu grunts, staring forward stoically. Miki whimpers; I look again, he's fidgeting.

Kahu brought us here for serious observation and ignores the self-important leprechaun. After a few moments, Kahu relents, sighs, and nods, continuing to stare at proceedings below.

Miki prances forward. Standing stiffly, extending his arms in a grand manner, he declaims in a thin, high-pitched voice:

> Facing each other in a formal game,
> Lined up on a medieval battle plain.
> Close quarter duel tests champions' mettle,
> Sides will wait before launching the battle.
> It's about 'manhood' and showing courage.
> Word and gesture taunts evoke mindless rage,
> Probe for weakness, locate sacrifices,
> Defiling dead, without graves suffices.

Strutting to the ridge's edge, Miki peeks back, seeking assurance he's impressed us. His descriptions subdued my thrill of being here. I enjoy pretend war play; toy soldiers don't experience pain. Miki has introduced horrible reality. He sits, crosses his legs, and becomes engrossed in watching instead of discoursing for a change.

I am on a trip into old-time Hawai'i. Kahu provides background information and encourages me to express thoughts.

He explains the situation: "This level unbroken plain, or *kahului*, allows the main body of solders to assume the crescent form taking shape. Those wishing to be first to reach the enemy covet the endpoints. Opposing forces will draw up in a line against each other."

It resembles a scene from the Peloponnesian Wars, twenty-four centuries earlier. *The Book of Knowledge* described how, in 460 B.C., the Spartan infantry-based army fought in phalanx formation, advancing in close rank before the Macedonians. Stamina and pushing ability were what counted; man-to-man, soldiers thrust back the enemy.

Kahu continues: "Attah, this battle is between your relative, the chief of Kaua'i and O'ahu—he's the defender—and the chief of Hawai'i—he is the invader. These Kāne'ohe plains are ideal for forming mass assaults. If they were on a scrub-covered or broken area, soldiers would be grouped into small units to accommodate the lay of the land."

"What year is it?" I ask.

"It is 1731. Your famous ancestor Kuali'i has been dead for eight years; that's his son and successor Pelei'oholani on the battlefield. Kuali'i won battles in Hilo, on the island of Hawai'i, but never exercised sovereignty there. Chief Alapa'i of Hawai'i is afraid Pelei'oholani may claim those rights. He's going to strike first and demonstrate his power by conquering O'ahu. Several thousand warriors from Kaua'i arrived by canoe to fight on Pelei'oholani's side."

"Who're the men in costumes?"

"High-ranking chiefs. Pelei'oholani is in the middle of the crescent to our left. You can identify him by the long feather cloak he's wearing that almost touches the ground. It shows he's a king."

I nod.

"*Aliʻi koa*—royal warriors—and high-placed *kanaka* on each side wear feather capes and ornate helmets."

I nod again.

"Men next to Peleiʻoholani hold his identifying standard—the *kahili*. Tufts of trimmed and splayed feathers top its staff.

"Attendants to Alapaʻi, the *mōʻī* on the other side of the field, hold that chief's identifying symbol. It is a *pūloʻuloʻu,* a staff surmounted by a *kapa*-covered ball."

Enemy king Alapaʻi stands in the middle of a cluster. Chief's helmets, on both sides, resemble Spartans' helmets; those had a crest arching from front to back. I saw illustrations in *The Book of Knowledge.*

I say, "Chiefs look like Spartans."

"Attah, you will meet a person experienced with that country and century. She says Hawaiian designs are original. Her husband's huge Persian army wiped out a small army of Spartans at Thermopylae in 480 B.C. At banquets, King Xerxes declared, 'Persian might is right.' She says he took a mouthful of wine and spat into Spartan king Leonidas' helmet. A Babylonian eunuch held it as a cuspidor.

"Queen Esther studied the helmet's design. She says Spartans created their helmets' decorative arch with horsehair. Hawaiians decorate their helmets' frame with interwoven yellow and red feathers. The helmet arch makes royal figures appear taller."

I think, *If Queen Esther is over two thousand and four hundred years old, she must resemble a mummy!*

Kahu explains what's happening below.

"The *mō'ī*—the king—holds the center during the advance. Brightly colored feathers on his cloak and helmet make him easy to spot. Being able to glance up and see he is still in command reassures his warriors."

"Who's walking forward?" I ask. "What's he carrying?"

"Pelei'oholani's priest holds a branch from a *hau* tree. Alapa'i's priest does the same thing on the other side of the field. Each kahuna will push his branch upright into the ground as a favorable omen; neither side will interfere with the other's symbol. The kahuna knocks the branch down if his side recognizes defeat. Ceremony was then an important part of warfare.

"The standard bearer for the Hawai'i chief is coming forward. You can't distinguish what he's holding from here. It's a carved staff; the tuft of feathers on top is a sacred emblem."

To the echoing sound of conch shell trumpets, opposing armies close within range of one another.

I ask, "Why has just one warrior stepped forward from Pelei'oholani's army?"

"He's a champion wanting to challenge an opponent to an individual skirmish. Ah, a respondent has approached him."

Kahu explains: "Pelei'oholani's warrior is using wordplay to destroy the opponent's morale. He's making obscene gestures, insulting his opponent's manhood."

"Why'd he throw down his weapon?"

"Now he's taunting, urging the opponent to fight weaponless. He intends to use his hands in *lua*—the art of breaking bones. He stands weaponless in front of the opposing army and its champion to demonstrate that he is *ʻōlohe lua*—the most proficient class of warrior. Kauaʻi teachers are famous for this secret knowledge. Their warriors can inflict a fatal blow with their bare hands.

"Look—the Hawaiʻi warrior is charging the Kauaʻi champion—his dagger is extended. He's ready to strike!"

I see movements, evidently parries. Seconds later, the Hawaiʻi opponent lies on the ground in a twisted position.

The Hawaiʻi front line stands still. Perhaps its men are looking on in shock? Two of Peleiʻoholani's warriors rush forward to pick up and carry away the fallen warrior.

Kahu says excitedly, "This means Peleiʻoholani's priest will have 'the *lehua*,' the first warrior downed on the field of battle. That Hawaiʻi man will be a sacrifice!"

He points to the hill opposite us. "Peleiʻoholani's priest will kill him over there on a rock for all to see. This is an omen of great fortune for warriors of Oʻahu and Kauaʻi."

Several individuals from the combined Oʻahu-Kauaʻi group advance toward the line of the enemy, pointing with spears; some are slinging stones.

"What are they doing?"

"They are intimidating, probing for strengths and weaknesses. They want two more victims for sacrifice. Three is their priest's magic number.

"Everything is one-on-one now—tests of individual manhood. Skirmishers will withdraw once the required sacrificial victims are obtained. And then the full-fledged battle will commence.

"Aha! Peleiʻoholani's men have captured two Hawaiʻi warriors. They're dragging them from the field, taking them to the priest! Pelei'oholani's massed army is taunting their opponents, who may fall for it."

Hawai'i warriors throw a salvo of spears. Many fall short. Pelei'oholani's warriors recover the spears, run forward, and simultaneously hurl them back.

"Watch for what Pelei'oholani orders. He learned warfare from his father. Your ancestor Kuali'i *never* lost a battle."

O'ahu-Kaua'i troops advance in line toward the Hawai'i army holding long pike-like spears aimed chest high.

"The *pololū* used en masse under skilled command is an ideal weapon for broaching or wedging a breach in an opponent's line. The point man at the front of this wedge is called the *maka,* or 'eye.' That position allows him to be the first to reach the enemy—a great honor. Once a breakthrough is achieved, fighting quickly shifts to fierce hand-to-hand combat at close quarters. Warriors use daggers and staves.

"See those warriors running down the crest of the hill, coming onto the field? They're Pelei'oholani's reserves. This battle has turned into melee, an interlocked mass of warriors. Reserves will reinforce the battle line. Look to your far right, beyond us: Some of Pelei'oholani's warriors have crept behind the enemy, seeking to cut off any retreat."

Those warriors include bare-breasted women in short skirts. I can tell from here!

A group of O'ahu-Kaua'i warriors rolls boulders down the hill toward the back lines of the Hawai'i army.

"I can't see the Hawai'i chief."

"It is hard to distinguish friend from foe once a melee begins," Kahu explains. "That's why an army identifies cohorts by types of tattoos—with geometric patterns over a shoulder, under the length of an arm or leg, over the chest, or in bands around the ankle or wrists. A chief can be spotted by his bright yellow or red feather cape and helmet. He's expected to move forward aggressively.

"A single battle can rage on for hours or drag on for days, with armies dividing and shifting territory."

"What happens to the defeated chief?"

"If a truce can't be arranged before the battle is completely lost, the *ali'i*—should he be spared from death—could lose all of his possessions, including the family genealogical chant that sets him apart. A defeated chief becomes part of the general populace, a *maka'āinana*."

"What about an ordinary warrior on the lost side?"

"Those spared may be become *kauwā*, or slaves—an untouchable class living apart from the rest of Hawaiian society. They become laborers or join a pool of persons to be used as human sacrifices. Heaviest losses occur when an opponent's forces collapse and are on the run. Hunting down a broken enemy's forces can go on for weeks. Victors bury their dead. Bodies of the vanquished are left for devouring by dogs and hogs, or to rot."

Warriors stop fighting as a procession forms on the left.

"Here comes a truce ambassador for Alapa'i."

A man holding a young banana tree advances toward Pelei'oholani from the rear of the Hawai'i army. Others follow, carrying green ti leaves.

The man with the tree prostrates himself before the Oʻahu-Kauaʻi chief, then stands, evidently making a declaration. Peleiʻoholani, appearing to agree, nods his head, then extends and raises his arms. Warriors from both sides put weapons on the ground and walk toward each other. Each bends his head toward a person he'd been trying to kill.

"What's going on, Kahu?"

"The battle is over. Former enemies are giving each other a *honi,* the traditional embrace—mutual touching of foreheads and noses and exchanges of breath. Warriors will then leave the battlefield."

We'd heard a general roar from the two armies when they advanced toward each other. Now high-pitched screams rise from a crowd running on the field from behind each army. They kneel beside fallen warriors.

"What's going on?"

"*Mahu* from both sides are helping those lying on the ground. They follow warriors, take care of their physical needs, cook, assist wounded, and bury the dead."

"Not warriors? Aren't they sissies?"

Kahu won't allow my snide comment to pass. He lectures me: "*Mahu* are important people, Attah! Some fight fiercely as warriors. Others provide comfort before and after battle. *Mahu* keep away loneliness and fear. Every Hawaiian has a purpose: Both male and female *mahu* are valued and loved. *Mahu* help care for children and instruct the young. They assist within the family and look after the aged. They create beautiful things, contribute to our culture, enhance and preserve it. Everyone is a *kanaka*—a human being. *That is something you need to learn.*"

Kahu spoke sincerely, not harshly. I am shamed and will remember that *every person has a purpose.*

I change the subject quickly: "What'll happen to the Hawai'i chief?"

"A peace has been negotiated, so he won't be harmed. Both sides went through rituals and formal battle discussions in advance. This mode of warfare will change over the next fifty years; sometime I will explain the evolution. But for now, your ancestor allows Alapa'i to withdraw to Maui. Back there, he continues to be aggressive and creates a rebellion. Pelei'oholani goes to Maui to settle it. He defeats Alapa'i, who, once again, asks for peace.

"Alapa'i returns to the island of Hawai'i and counters a rebellion *against him* this time. After many battles, that warfare-loving chief is overthrown.

"Tomorrow you'll observe your ancestor Kuali'i. I explained that he is Pelei'oholani's father."

He looks toward Miki, who was subdued when fighting began but not now. Miki turns, grins, and bounces up and down excitedly now that all has ended well and declaims,

> I prefer naked warriors in make up:
> Those completely nude men and women Picts,
> Blue paint covering their face and body,
> Fighting side-by-side, looking s-o-o bawdy!
> Stunning the Romans, and never losing,
> Distilling whisky for happy boozing.

Then, with a swagger, he says,

> Grandma knows of Scotland's blue belles and boys
> Turning the Roman soldiers into toys.

She's an "Armstrong," whose coat of arm's a fist,
A bent arm muscle, pops up just like this!

Flexing his tiny left bicep, Miki points to it, wanting me to realize he knows everything—it's pixie one-upmanship.

Kahu places his hand on my back, and instantly we're at the eucalyptus tree behind the abandoned Kona Hospital. Kahu nods good-bye. He and Miki disappear in the guava bushes. I walk down to the former nurse quarters where Mother and I live.

2. Meeting Menehune

Excited by my trip into the past, I wrote about that while it was fresh on my mind—instead of beginning my journal ten days ago on April 1, 1942, when I first met menehune--I will start doing so right now.

Mother gave me this nice writing book she thinks I'm using as my "secret diary." We agreed not even she can see what I write between its covers. If loose-leaf, instead of bound, I could've moved the sequence around. In that case, if I hadn't reacted to the moment, like a kid, this journal would've started with the retrospective and explanatory writing I'm now doing after catching on to sequencing.

I am ten years old. Menehune, Hawai'i's magical people, take me on adventures into Hawai'i's ancient past. During the past seven years I've learned to associate with those whom others don't see.

This began with "pictures," similar to those Hilda Doolittle described in a poem:

An adult told a child:
"People don't dream until they're ten."
The child responded: "But I had a five-year-old one."
The adult asked: "How did it come?"

The child explained: "It didn't come. It was there. It was a picture. It was real!"

That's how it happened to me. Over time, pictures evolved into complex dramas. They continue to be real, expanding as I grow.

While transitioning from one foster home after another, I compensated with imaginary affinities. They never left me. Replaying what I read kept imaginary friends in my head. I imitated authors' language in what I said.

Robert Louis Stevenson had such friends. He created his own world and even wrote a poem—"The Unseen Playmate"—who loves to be little, hates to be big.

Gradually, book-by-book, I entered the creative zone. *Why would one ever want to leave such a comforting, safe, secret shield?*

At age eight I returned to Honolulu, Territory of Hawai'I after four years of living in foster homes in Washington State and Los Angeles. My grandparents, who lived in Kaimuki, a Honolulu suburb, took me in. After Pearl Harbor was attacked, my grandparents sent me to Kona on the island of Hawai'i to be with my mother who had just transferred there after working at the Leper Colony on the Island of Molokai. They thought I'd be safer there because Japanese invaders were going to tear up O'ahu.

Aunty Kalei Lyman, a Hilo resident, was the first to suggest my affinity for menehune. She knew everything about anything and chuckled while explaining some of it to me.

"The name of your Kona village, Kealakekua, means 'Pathway of the Gods,'" she began one evening as we sat on her big *pūneʻe*. From that couch on her porch, I looked down on gardenias and pikake wafting fragrance up to us.

"The real name should actually be Kealekeʻakua. Akua is the word for god or gods. But when haoles— the white people in charge—made maps and signs they left out an 'a'. The Hawaiian they concocted translates into *the pathway along the back.* Only persons fluent in Hawaiians catch on to this aberration. The language is disappearing. But getting back to the akua, the ghosts of gods who are around there.

"On moonlight nights, a chief leads a procession of the dead through that area."

"It must be true," I responded. "Mother let anxious, whining Pat out of the house one moonlight night shortly before I arrived. He sped down the hospital road, suddenly yelped, and disappeared."

"Ancient Hawaiians loved dog meat," Aunty Kalei commented.

Wicked thing to say! But only Mother liked Pat. A very protective bull terrier, he snarled at everyone, lifted his leg and urinated everywhere and anytime to demonstrate his feelings. Pat bit anyone but her without provocation. He nipped me twice when she brought him to Honolulu.

According to Aunty, menehune aren't like ghostly night marchers. These industrious little people work together, building walls, temples, and ponds in a single night! To keep on their good side, she hung a bunch of bananas in an open-air basement for them to eat.

"Sometimes you hear them chattering away in the bushes," she confided. Although never seeing any, Aunty seemed confident they were out there. She thought I might have an affinity for them.

"Kuali'i, your ancestor, associated with menehune. And *you are* a little different, Arthur."

Youngsters on the island of Hawai'i were taught to believe what Tutu and Aunty say. I was ready for whoever or whatever came along.

On my eucalyptus perch, I daydreamed about two favorite authors who once stayed at the Hilo Boarding School. Leaving Hawai'i, after experiencing a snowy winter in New York's Adirondack Mountains, Robert Louis Stevenson visited an island in the Marquesas. "I shall have the material—strange stories and characters, cannibals, ancient legends, old island poetry," he wrote in the book *In the South Seas*. Sickly all his life, RLS lived to be forty-four years old. Now he lies in Samoa, where he longed to be.

Mark Twain bridged a thirteen-century gap in one night: Hank Morgan went to bed in nineteenth-century Hartford, Connecticut, where Colt pistols and Sharps rifles were made. He woke up in sixth-century Camelot to associate with King Arthur and the Knights of the Round Table, who fought with sharp implements.

Wish I could visit ancient Hawai'i the Twain way— simply close my eyes and go back into time.. I'd like to experience things in *real depth*. Mother spent her early youth here. She told me stories about some of the places we traveled by. While driving past a lava field, I asked why the top of a stone church was stuck in it. She explained, "Pele destroyed all but that tower because she enjoyed hearing the bell ring as flowing lava carried the church away."

Another time, she pointed to where lava left an open spot—it stopped and went around a rundown house, leaving it in the middle of an overgrown yard, surrounded by lava—an island in a lava sea.

Mother described, "Villagers refused Pele arrowroot when she appeared disguised as an old woman." Arrowroot, a starch with gelling properties, was used as a thickening agent for making *haupia,* the wonderful coconut cream pudding. Angry over being rebuffed, Pele destroyed that village with hot lava.

Mother explained this phenomenon: "Pele left *that* house untouched because the family living there shared arrowroot with her."

Ohia trees eventually rise from lava; roots take hold, cracks appear in lava rock, other plants start. Eventually, maybe centuries later, lava becomes soil. Volcanic eruptions continue on Hawai'i, newest of the Hawaiian Islands, because this is where Pele lives. We drove through miles of barren lava plains where only ohia trees grew.

A red ohia blossom, called 'lehua,' is Pele's favorite flower. Mother said, "Dare to pick it, she'll make rain fall on you."

She augmented what Aunty Kalei told me about menehune snd told the story of a golden lehua tree. She'd heard it from Mary Kawena Pukui of Ka'ū, her friend from girlhood: "A scruffy little tree in the forest cried because it had no blooms like other beautiful trees. Seeing the tears, menehune bowed their heads one night and said a blessing. When the tree woke up the next day, it had special golden blossoms, whereas other trees had only ordinary red ones!"

This sounded like a Christian children's book story—especially the part about menehune praying to bring the unusual blossoms into being. Any stories I heard about menehune were episodic: "How something happened." These weren't like "Once upon a time" fairy tales that I enjoyed for depth and personalities.

Aunty Kalei talked about menehunes' maniacal determination, how so quickly they built ponds, walls, and *heiau*. Sparse stories about menehune identified them as hardworking—shadows of players on a brief stage, without personality. What little I heard didn't satisfy my curiosity. Why weren't menehune like fairies everywhere else?

Hawai'i has legends about Pele, Maui, and other larger-than-life personalities. What about the little enchanted folk who might be all around? Cohorts are described almost everywhere else.

Irish have leprechauns and banshees—the latter seem like Pele, who appears as a beautiful woman or a hag. Banshees dress in gray and assume other shapes, as does Pele.

All ethnicities have "changelings," creatures taking the place of a sweet human infant. They are ill-tempered, causing parents to wonder "What happened?"

Slavics have Baba Yaga—a crafty witch who rides a broomstick—as did the Wicked Old Witch in *The Wizard of Oz* movie.

In addition to Tomte, the Santa Claus who came to my Los Angeles foster home, Scandinavians have Pookah—goblins that cause harm and mischief.

Even Iceland has many types of elves. Hidden people and invisible beings inhabit that island nation.

Fairies elsewhere had personalities and were known to interact between their world and ours, unlike placid menehune who avoid humans.

Why aren't menehune like other fairies?

The Grimm Brothers' dramas center on interplay between fairy folk and humans.

The Seven Dwarfs recognized good omens, saved Snow White, and gave her advice she was too air-headed to observe: "When we are away in the mines, you must not open the door." Rumpelstiltskin, ugly as a wart, a dwarf with a no-sex voice, spun gold out of straw and danced and sang his name. Mother Gothal wanted no one but her to touch Rapunzel, expressing her belief that a woman who loves a woman is forever young.

A king had a christening for his daughter Briar Rose; having just twelve gold plates, he invited only twelve fairies. The angry thirteenth fairy made an evil prophecy: The king, servants, and his beautiful daughter went into a trance. A fence grew around Briar Rose, but one hundred years later a prince broke through, awakening her with a kiss. Iron Hans, the wild man to whom only a young prince was kind, became redeemed as a proud king who had been bewitched. The Frog, who retrieved the princess' golden ball and was kissed as a reward, turned out to be a handsome prince with kind eyes and gentle hands who was a friend of sorrow.

Hidden significances within Grimm's German tales perhaps piqued my prepubescent curiosity. Mother's friend Dr. Mildred Mendelson pointed that out. She is a psychiatrist employed by the Territory of Hawai'i and helps some of Mother's clients. I've heard her mention Dr. Sigmund Freud's work; she seems to enjoy talking with me. My word choices sometimes cause her eyebrows to rise—then she laughs merrily. Dr. Mendelson is from North Carolina; I've never known anyone who sounds like her. Her drawl stretches a sentence so far that sometimes I'm ready to answer before she's finished.

At least Grimms' personalities aren't shallow—nor are the folks in Lewis Carroll's *Alice in Wonderland*. If "Freudian," as Dr. Mendelson suggests, they certainly are varied and interesting—unlike Hawai'i's bland menehune, lacking in personality.

Is there undisclosed intrigue in the menehune world? Does it have a dark and bright side?

How exciting if, like Mark Twain's Hank Morgan, I woke up in a different, exciting time period and met unusual beings!

What if Peter Pan guided me through Hawai'i as he did Wendy in England and elsewhere? Is there such a place as Neverland? How did the Lost Boys get there? Does Hawai'i's unknown world contain more than ordinary people know?

The tree's menthol odor is soothing my sinuses. The cooling breeze is drying my perspiration-dampened aloha shirt. Musing is making me drowsy. Thinking about otherworld people is relaxing and I feel mentally released. Maybe I'm experiencing what Dr. Mendelson describes as "a transference." But to whom or to what am I being transferred?

I hear "Psst! Hey, Attah."

Imagination? Dr. Mendelson mentioned that some patients "hear voices."

"Attah." Then louder, "Attah, come down. We must talk!"

Peering down, I see a small beckoning person who resembles Queequeg—as Rockwell Kent drew him for Melville's *Moby Dick*. He has muscular arms, a brawny chest, a jutting hooked nose—unusual on a Hawaiian face. His head is shaven, except for an upright top lock of black hair. He's holding a primitive-looking canoe paddle, slightly taller than he is.

I don't feel intimidated; his deep, resonant voice sounds friendly, and *he did* use my nickname.

Sliding down the tree's stringy bark, I march toward him with an authoritarian knightly stride. I stop short in realization: *He is wearing my blue shorts!* They disappeared from our clothesline. Mother scolded me for "misplacing them."

Although skinny and small for my age, I tower over this dark-brown guy, who's about the height of a four- or five-year-old. A big grin makes him appear genuinely pleased to see me. Instinctively, I grin back.

My shorts are too big for him. He tied them around his waist with a piece of rope—probably cut from a dangling end of our clothesline.

"We see you prepare for attack. You have warrior blood!"

That cryptic statement is something I'd never heard: "warrior blood?" I feel an excited tingle but stare blankly, hiding my feelings: insensitivity training. I've had years of experience.

He continues: "You are the thirteenth-generation descendent of Kuali'i. I offer my respect."

Bending his head, he looks down as if meditating. Politely, I start to imitate his gesture. He retorts quickly, sharply: "No! No bow! *Not pono for you!*"

Resuming a kindly tone, he continues, "I've watched your ancestor perform many feats and have forgiven him for having owls chase us."

My bewilderment causes him to grin.

"I am Na Kahu. Call me 'Kahu.' It means 'teacher.' That's what I'll be. You'll learn about Hawaiians. It's your destiny."

He must have brought the little green ti leaf-wrapped package lying next to the eucalyptus tree. Picking it up, opening it, Kahu removes a brownish pudding. Taking a knife from the pocket of my blue shorts—lifted, I suspect, from our kitchen—he cuts the pudding into sections.

"Ah Soong made this v-e-r-y good *kūlolo* from taro, coconut milk, arrowroot, and sugar. We'll celebrate before starting your lessons."

The "celebration" consists of him popping *kūlolo* into his mouth. I hold onto the serving he hands me. Some of King Arthur's knights received food from an unknown "amiable host." Eating it, they fell under a spell and woke up chained in a prison.

This Kahu guy won't enchant me!

The pudding makes him jolly, so I eat some. Cool, moist, and sweet, it gives me a quick burst of energy. I eagerly scoop up and swallow the rest. Now I'm ready for whatever comes next! I realize Kahu is a menehune, one of the enchanted little people Aunty Kalei mentioned. She's never seen one—now I have.

Sidney's grandmother knows about menehune, too. We gather around her as she tells stories to Sidney, his seven brothers, eight sisters, and me. Sidney, in my Konawaena class, lives in Kailua, several miles from Hospital Hill. Mother allows me to ride the school bus to and from his home, and we spend weekends together once a month or so.

His tutu reinforced what Aunty Kalei told me: "Menehune can't be seen because they come out only at night and shy away from humans."

But here is Kahu: chipper and chatty, trotting up a steep volcanic hill, moving readily through dense bushes, leading me somewhere on a sunny afternoon.

3. Into Unseen Hawai'i

Kahu zigzags beyond the guava bushes, using his paddle to push branches away. The landscape changes dramatically: Temperature becomes cooler, tall trees form closed canopies, air is moist, puffy clouds—*'ōpua*—rise above what I realize is a rain forest.

I hear chirping birds of all colors looking like those Aunty Kalei Lyman paints: red, orange, yellow, green, and indigo—those having splashes of bright blue feathers make piercing, cheeping sounds. A thought: *Maybe a Lyman musician will create birdsongs as nice as what I hear—something novel.*

Little brown birds with white collars, resembling the kind Rev. Miller wears, are extremely bold and curious. They fly close, sit on trees, look us over, and whistle loudly.

"They're telling you their name," says Kahu. "Hear it? *'El-e-pai-o.*"

Sure enough. It's *exactly* what they're singing.

Kahu explains: "Old Hawai'i canoe builders watch for *'elepaio* when seeking trees to carve. *'Elepaio* are insect eaters; if they're pecking a tree, that means it's filled with bugs. Men don't waste their time cutting down that tree. Insects will have bored holes in it."

I sing, *"El-e-pai-o,"* imitating their sound. They warble back.

Tall bananas and white and yellow blooming ginger are in profusion. Orchids, ferns, and liana vines grow on other plants. Tree ferns are prominent in the undergrowth, and broadleaf plants surround us, some resembling Grandpa's huge philodendron. Seeing me awed by the dense foliage, eager to poke through to study it, Kahu walks slowly, guiding me.

He points to masses of a gray, beardlike plant with threadlike stems and leaves: "That is *hinahina,* the flower of Kahoʻolawe. It may look dead, but it is alive; we use it for medicine. It's called 'Spanish moss' in English. Red berries on those little bushes are *ʻōhelo,* Pele's favorite treat. Ah Soong makes *ʻōhelo* jelly sauce." I surmise he will tell me about Ah Soong, who prepared *kūlolo* to lure me here.

"Those are *ʻōhiʻa ʻai,* called 'mountain apples' in English," he says, pointing to trees having red fruit hanging within easy reach. "They're luscious when eaten right off the tree. Ah Soong also salts the fruit, then dries it in the sun as a savory treat."

We're in a place like Shangri-La. That is the name of James Hilton's "Paradise" in his book, *Lost Horizon.* I have never seen such lush natural beauty. My senses need to see, touch, and smell so I can become involved with it.

Kahu walks slowly by my side; I'm absorbing *everything.*

Red and pink torch ginger blossoms at the end of long stalks rise to over twice my height. These extend from clumps of big green leaves, resembling *kāhili*—symbols of royalty.

Hearing water flowing, I push through the *kāhili* ginger and see several small ponds; lehua blossoms float on them.

"This is our protein farm," Kahu explains. "*Oʻopu* live in these *oʻopu ʻai lehua*—the Hawaiian name for upland ponds. White folks call these freshwater fish 'bass.' We feed them and look for fatties under patches of watercress to spear with sticks. We catch *ʻōpae*—shrimp—in streams above here and put them into the ponds. One shrimp fills a menehune's little *opu*. See those little black shells hanging on the rocks just below the water surface? They are *pipipi;* the English term is 'small mollusk.' Ah Soong steams them with leeks. He says, 'They're menehune-size escargot.' Very tasty, particularly with the smidgens of wild garlic he adds to a dipping sauce."

Yes, I am in Shangri-La, under the *ʻōpua,* where *oʻopu, ʻōpae,* and *ʻopelu* grow and *pipipi* becomes escargot.

I breathe easily and have no difficulty keeping up with Kahu. We come to an open area he identifies as "our savanna." It is flat grassland, about half the size of Konawaena's playing field. At its outskirts is a cluster of trees with hanging yellow fruit.

"Those pomelo are originally from China," Kahu explains. "Ah Soong brought the seeds. Pomelos taste like grapefruit but sweeter. Ah Soong puts sugar juice, salt, and ginger on the rind and dries it. He gives it to us to chew on like candy. He makes a similar treat from mango seeds. You'll meet him now."

Grinning, Ah Soong walks somewhat awkwardly toward us from the entrance of a grotto, wearing blue pajamas and a round black cap. Ah Soong's pigtail reaches to about the middle of his back. His thin chin whiskers are about three inches long. Stopping four feet away, then bowing, Ah Soong addresses me in a high-pitched voice.

"Chun Hung, your ancestor, and I travel from Macao. Chief Kaiana come to Canton. We return on the English boat Iphigenia in 1788. I help your ancestor operate his sugar mill on Maui, also work in the Honolulu store, bank, hotel, and restaurant."

A concise speech; does he think I'm naïve enough to believe he did all that over 150 years ago?

Adhering to ingrained behavior, I respond politely, "Thank you for the delicious pudding."

Ah Soong smiles, turns, and shuffles backward.

He's informed me of a Chinese ancestor—one of Hawai'i's earliest entrepreneurs. Chinese blood in the family? Another thing Grandpa never mentioned.

4. Leprechaun Miki

"**H**ere comes Miki," Kahu says enthusiastically. A red-haired, light-skinned little man comes out of the grotto. He removes and sets down a tall green hat; he's wearing a green coat, knickers, and a belt with a big buckle. Miki turns rapid cartwheels as he approaches. Stopping where Ah Soong just stood, he mirthfully shouts:

Greetings R-r-r-ath!

And then he goes into a little act:

Miki the Pixie of leprechaun fame
Here to tell you what he knows of your name.

Bowing from the waist, speaking in a lilting tenor, rolling his r's, he continues:

In Ireland a rath is a fortress
Around which wee folk dance during darkness:
Tiny fairy footsteps ringing a rath
Are signs of good luck for all on its path.

> From me you will learn of the "Good People"
> Who can appear big as well as little.
> Live in raths forever, have houses there,
> In different forms they can go everywhere!

Placing his arms to his side like a soldier, he hums and does an Irish step dance—a short interval of jumps, hops, and side steps. Finishing with a grin, he resumes his speech, without the rolled "r" affectation:

> I'm with your family since eight-hundred,
> For with King Alfred, Lymans are numbered.
> Sixteen-hundred, America we came,
> Eighteen-hundred, to Hawai'i, the same name.
> Personal lore deserves some exploring;
> We little guys will help with your knowing.
> I've lots to share with explaining for you,
> Just rely on me and we'll see you through!

Miki pauses briefly, seeming of a mind to continue step dancing. Grinning, he shrugs his shoulders instead and steps back a few paces.

I've entered a phantasmagoria of weird little people having the fey look of the nineteenth-century characters John Tenniel illustrated for Lewis Carroll's *Alice in Wonderland*.

This Irishman claims to having been around in the ninth century—and references my family's Caucasian roots in a lighthearted way. I don't know about anything he's said.

King Alfred? Fairies dancing around a Rath?

Has *kūlolo* made me *lolo*? Am I hallucinating?

Kahu comments, "Other menehune will tell you more."

Miki picks up and puts on his tall hat and strolls back to the grotto entrance.

Kahu explains quietly: "Miki hung around London's Globe Theater before stowing away to the South Pacific. He became stagestruck. It's why he speaks that way. Miki shadowed William Shakespeare—being invisible, of course. The Bard had Miki in mind when creating the elf Puck for *A Midsummer Night's Dream* because at night Miki breathed such thoughts into his ears—at least, *that's* what Miki claims."

Now I understand. Miki plays his alter ego's role. His indefinite phrases are to mystify me as he pretends to be

> That wanderer of the night who could put a girdle
> 'Round the earth in forty minutes.

Shakespeare's Puck observed, "Oh what fools these mortals be!" I'm going to listen carefully so this guy's fast-talking brogue doesn't pass over my head. He won't beguile *me* into being a fool!

I reflect on my introduction to Shakespeare. Belden, Sam's oldest brother, took me to see *A Midsummer Night's Dream* at the University of Hawai'i. Stage electrician for the university's drama program, Belden aspired to attend Yale School of Drama. Belden's dream became a war casualty. He enlisted in the Army Engineer Corps to do lighting work on airfields.

Belden took me to the university's Christmas pageant dress rehearsal. I sat behind a lovely angel taking an offstage break. That's when I realized guardian angels are *beautiful*.

I cut angel wings from a newspaper the next day and wore them around the house. Grandma said, disapprovingly, "Humans can't anoint themselves as angels."

I threw away the wings.

"Harrumph!" Kahu ends my daydreaming. "The main reason I brought you here is because of the person you'll now meet."

A sarcastic paraphrase pops instantly to mind and I almost say, *And from what century will be he?*

This tongue-in-cheek attitude began after I read Mark Twain's two adventure books about *Tom Sawyer* and *Huckleberry Finn*. I haven't yet learned how far to go with this kind of behavior; I just don't realize when it's inappropriate. "Smart talk" lurks in my head—sometimes, I just blurt! I caught myself and have my tongue in check this time; don't want to make a poor impression on Kahu, who says he's my mentor.

Uncle Sam gave me *Shadows of Blue and Gray,* my introduction to Ambrose Bierce, also an asthma sufferer. After I read that Civil War book, Uncle Sam gave me Bierce's *Devil's Dictionary: The Cynic's Wordbook*. I enjoy Bierce's sassiness, but I shouldn't emulate him. He mysteriously disappeared from Pancho Villa's army. A shooting squad may have shut him up.

Kahu said he will teach me about Hawaiians. Perhaps by understanding their background, practices, and mores I may become forgiving, amiable, and more Hawaiian. Being verbally quick, critical, and cutting is fun, but sarcasm can be hurtful. I must recognize boundaries and know when not to cross them.

5. How Japan Will Win

Leaving daydreaming, I see a thin Japanese elf in a white uniform standing outside of the grotto. A sailor's cap sits atop his bushy hair. Marching crisply forward, he positions himself where Ah Soong and Miki stood. Clicking his heels, he barks out in a high-pitched voice: "I am Rising Sun. Your war preparations are useless!"

He glares at me from behind round, wire-rimmed glasses. I stand rigid, hoping his insult didn't make me flush.

Miki pipes up from the background:

> Rising Sun ain't diplomatic a'tall,
> Arrogance 'tis his prelude to a fall.

"Tell him your story," Kahu directs.

With a condescending tone, Rising Sun begins.

"*Your king* wanted Hawai'i to be associated with Japan. During his visit to Japan in 1881, *your* King Kalākaua suggested his niece Princess Ka'iulani marry our Prince Akihito to forge a bond between Japanese and Hawaiian royalty. This could not be, because our Honorable Prince already had a prearranged marriage commitment.

"Your king urged Japan to lead a federation of Asian nations of which Hawai'i would become a member."

I interrupt: "Why'd Tokyo decline?"

"We were already there," he sniffs. "Our national policy built a strong military, strengthened industry, we became a world power through victories in the Sino-Japanese and Russo-Japanese wars, and we annexed Korea."

Disgusted by arrogance, I snarl, "How'd *you* get here?"

"The *Ondo* brought me to Hilo in 1937. I left the ship because my help was needed in Kona."

A sixth-grader, whom I think of as "Sweet Sumiko," told our classmates that Japanese naval vessels began making regular visits to Hawai'i in 1876. "The Japanese admiral Togo Heihachiro became so popular that a brand of sake brewed in Hilo was named after him."

Sumiko explained why: "In 1905 the Russian fleet had traveled halfway around the world to attack Japan at its gateway. Togo's fleet wiped out the Tsar's armada within hours, boosting Japanese national pride enormously. For the first time, Asians had defeated Caucasians. Lots of sake drinking over that!"

Her father, Kona's sheriff, was invited to Hilo's gala reception for the *Ondo* and *Erimo* Japanese training ships.

"Maybe what you really want to know is *why* I'm here," Rising Sun sneers, realizing my attention is drifting.

Not liking his adversarial attitude, I snap back, as Huck Finn might do, "Okay. Why?"

Rising Sun is dogmatic: "All Asians will ultimately benefit from our crusade to reform China and build a New Order. I came here to help Japanese officials influence Hawai'i's 160,000 *doho* to help with our Holy War.

"Hawai'i's Nisei have been fighting for Japan against China since 1937. A steady flow of recruits in the second Sino-Japanese War came from the Kona community.

"Our foreign ministry believed Japanese-Americans should give half of their assets to support Japan's Holy War.

"I watched local Issei during the day. At night I whispered what I saw into the ears of Japanese agents— who couldn't see me, of course. I penetrated their subconscious; they put my observations into reports and pressured people to do their part who were terrified by the inside knowledge I'd given agents. I was very busy." Rising Sun has a smug expression.

"Our holy war will cleanse Greater East Asia of Chiang Kai-shek, Mao and his Communists, and the Anglo-Saxons. We do this to build a Greater East Asia Co-Prosperity Sphere in which Asians can live and prosper under Imperial Japan's benevolent tutelage."

I wriggle my nose. He's saying things I don't understand. I respond angrily, "Was the Pearl Harbor attack part of your 'Holy War?'"

Rising Sun continues his rhetoric: "We attacked Pearl Harbor so Americans would lose their will to fight and agree to a peace on our terms. Japan would then control the western Pacific and Southeast Asia and carry out its destiny."

Closing his eyes, he softly and reverently says, "Pilots of our midget submarines surfaced to scatter cherry blossoms at the entrance to Pearl Harbor prior to arrival of the Imperial forces. These signified their wish to fight and die together. Cherry blossoms represent souls of fallen soldiers. They are symbols of death and reincarnation. Japanese warriors scatter as flowers on the skirmish, not sparing their lives. Their loyalty is firm as a rock."

This mystery voice he's started using is scarier! After pausing for effect, he resumes being arrogant, abrasive, and annoying.

"The new Kona Hospital's director is a *doho* who visited Japan in early 1941. During a broadcast from Tokyo to Honolulu, he stated, 'Japan is going to win!' He aimed his radio appeal specifically to local *doho,* saying, 'Hawai'i listeners, please explain to Americans that Japan is determined to construct a New World Order.'

"We didn't realize how weak resistance would be. We should have seized O'ahu while Americans were paralyzed with confusion."

Excitedly, he explains what is ahead: "We will assault this sparsely populated and undefended island of Hawai'i. The Big Island will become a giant aircraft carrier. We will construct airfields on cleared cane fields and over old lava flows. Hilo will become the base for the final drive on O'ahu, and the Imperial Navy will wrest control of the skies. Isolated and pummeled, O'ahu will fall to amphibious assault.

"We can attack America once we seize the Hawaiian Islands. Our aircraft carriers will move within range. The Pacific Coast will be exposed to bombardments by squadrons of the Rising Sun.

"Tokyo will be in a strong position to push the United States for a quick peace settlement once Hawai'i is in Japanese hands."

His recitation reflects *The Shape of Things to Come*, an H. G. Wells book I'm looking through. Overwhelmed, anxious, I turn toward Kahu: "I want to go home now. Uncle Sam's coming for dinner."

Rising Sun crisply executes a military-style "about face" and marches to the grotto.

Kahu points toward the trail that led us here. I follow him through the rain forest and then the guava bushes. I am very uneasy and tremulous.

At the clothesline, Kahu looks at me benevolently and says, "You have much to learn. Climb the eucalyptus tree when you want me to find you."

"Home" is only a few steps away. I will write everything down right now about the *New World Order* while able to remember what I've just learned.

6. Alienation

The army assigned Uncle Sam to special detail with the FBI. Here to interview Kona Issei, he sleeps in my room; I use the living room couch.

Seeing his blackjack on my dresser, I ask about it, and he shows me a .45 automatic pistol from the FBI— "Things I'll never need," he explains. Uncle Sam earned marksmanship medals while in the university's Reserve Officer Training Corps; the tip of a finger he lost wasn't on his shooting hand.

Mother visits aliens who have to choose between reparation to Japan or internment. I sometimes wait in her car while she talks; this duty makes her very sad. I think she welcomes my optimistic company.

An elderly couple being sent back to Japan on an exchange ship offered her the title to their home, which of course she refused. "It is un-Christian to take advantage of another's misfortune," she explained later.

I was invited in for soda and snacks at another house. The middle-aged couple showed me a decorative clear-glass jar containing liquid and an open oyster in which a large pearl "had grown." This treasure fascinated me. They wanted to give it to Mother. She wouldn't accept it.

I ask Uncle Sam about our island being invaded—not telling him how I came up with that idea. He describes a new Saddle Road between Mauna Kea and Mauna Loa volcanoes: "Anticipating an invasion, the CCC and U.S. Army Engineers are building an approximately 6.5-mile gravel roadway for access to its training area and a small airfield. The road will enable civilians and defenders to reach the other side of the island, going across instead of around the island. The fog there is very dense; low visibility will help persons trying to hide from the Japanese within the island's interior.

Uncle Sam mentions Uncle Albert's connection to this project on his home island.

I think but don't ask, *Won't the road create a shortcut for the Japanese army?*

I tell him about the Japanese red rising sun symbol painted on the eave of the house next to the poi factory, saying, "It should be painted over."

A couple of weeks later the rising sun is still there, but now it is bright blue. The owner was either extremely literal—painting "over" instead of painting "out"—or he is defiant.

My even thinking of the word "defiant" reveals the effect of Mark Twain, Ambrose Bierce, and wartime on my psyche. I'm getting cocky—not a good trait—probably because I don't have playmates to knock it out of me. Maybe by listening carefully to Kahu I can become amiable—maybe more Hawaiian.

Ihaven't journalized about menehune for a while. Uncle Sam and Mother are doing "alien" work. I ride with Mother during her sad calls. Uncle Sam and I talk about books at night. He gave me my early reading start. I'll explain later.

What if the poi factory owner finds out I ratted on him? I am frightened; the entire Pacific is about to fall under Japanese dominance. It's what Rising Sun said.

I whistle while tagging along with Mother to buy poi. I heard about doing that when passing a graveyard at night. Ghosts will concentrate on the music instead of on you.

Whistling is a smart precaution; after several visits, I feel calmer. People in the Japanese-owned poi factory don't realize *I'm* the one who contacted the FBI, aka Uncle Sam, and that's why their red sun turned blue.

After several visits, Mother comments that poi factory people are complimentary about my variety of music. "The Whistler's'" repertoire includes Antonin Dvorak's *Humoresque*, Johann Strauss' *Blue Danube Waltz,* and, of course, Sir Edward Elgar's *Pomp and Circumstance.* They're carryovers from violin lesson days now over; Kona doesn't have stringed instrument instructors.

Sam, finished with his Kona work, is returning to the army. He says, "I've been assigned to armored forces, will be going to the mainland—and then, who knows? I'm glad to be finished dealing with good people caught in a tight vise. Be polite to everyone, Arthur. Increase your vocabulary; use lots of words conveying warm, human thoughts. Slow down, don't be quick to make judgments that may turn out to be wrong."

Mother and Uncle's alien-nation work is over. Mostly alone again, I have time for menehune.

7. Japan's Hawai'i Kingdom

Wanting to know more of Japan's upcoming plans, I climb the eucalyptus tree. Hearing "Psst!" I slide down and follow Kahu.

At the savanna, the open field, I ask my new teacher, "Please, may I see Rising Sun?"

Kahu whistles like a boatswain. Impressive! *How does he do that?*

He beckons to Rising Sun peering from the grotto. Today that sailor boy leisurely walks toward us. Standing in a relaxed posture, smiling, he remarks, "I suppose you have more questions."

"Yes, I do. What are Japan's plans for Hawai'i?"

Reverting to the rigid posture he showed me the last time, Rising Sun begins a jingoistic lecture. Details and jargon are beyond my comprehension. Probably from overhearing Japanese officials, here is what he relates: "We will make Hawai'i self-sufficient. American exploiters made Hawai'i vulnerable and dependent on food imports."

He rattles off statistics and specifics: "Hawai'i grows 84% of its fruit, but the percentages of other foodstuffs grown locally are very low: rice 10%, dairy products 28%, fish 30%, eggs 40%, meat 41%, and vegetables 46%. Japan will remodel the Islands' agriculture.

"Hawai'i has forty-eight mills producing almost 9 million tons of cane sugar. Less than 400,000 tons are used locally; the rest goes to the mainland to make the Big Five richer. We will limit sugar cultivation, plant rice and taro instead, and we'll use neglected marginal lands to grow sweet potatoes. We will raise superior-quality pineapples and coffee to be consumed in Japan.

"We can convert over 90 percent of the cane fields into rice paddies and vegetable farms. Existing irrigation systems will provide water for rice fields and taro patches. Japanese are more productive than Chinese, who raise one rice crop annually. We can grow two!

"We will expand livestock raising and harvest sea kelp for cattle feed.

"By planting trees on hills and in mountainous area, we will lay the basis for a forestry industry to provide construction materials.

"Our garrison troops can help with harvests and other seasonal work."

Something else is on my mind: "Hawai'i is under martial law. Is that how Japan will rule Hawai'i?"

He responds as if addressing a large audience instead of just me: "We have ample experience restoring areas to native inhabitants: in Manchukuo, Inner Mongolia, and north China.

"We will reestablish the Hawaiian Kingdom. Princess Kawananakoa, leader of the anti-Roosevelt Republican Party, might be the head. Descendents of royal and princely families live on all of the main islands.

"Hawai'i will be freed from the American yoke, and the nostalgic past shall be revived under the Rising Sun flag!"

He seems especially smug about reviving Hawai'i's "nostalgic past." Evidently Rising Sun listens in on royalist cadres and Royal Society assemblages. He's absorbed their rhetoric and formed his own conclusions.

Not knowing what more to ask, I say, very sincerely, "Thank you for sharing that valuable information with me."

Smiling broadly, as if charmed, Rising Sun graciously responds, "We'll discuss more at some another time."

My psyciatrist friend, Dr. Mendelson, would describe Rising Sun's contradictory behavior as "schizophrenic."

He bows and returns to the grotto.

Ah Soong waves from the entrance, then steps aside for Rising Sun to enter. Now he walks toward us holding a bowl. Actually, he waddles.

Two young menehune wearing loincloths follow; one holds a handful of ti leaves, the other carries a green coconut. The assistants spread the leaves on the ground. Motioning for me to sit, Ah Soong takes a pair of chopsticks from the pocket of his pajama-like shirt, hands me a filled-to-the-brim coconut shell bowl, and presents the chopsticks with a bow.

"A treat for you, Attah. It is broil freshwater shrimp and slice tree fern shoots with lime juice dressing. I garnish with bits of roast *kukui* nuts."

The young menehune places the chilled drinking coconut next to me; the top and inner nut are sliced open.

I use the chopsticks eagerly; I love hearts of artichoke. Tree fern shoots are even better! I tell Ah Soong, "These blended flavors make my palate sing. Refreshing coconut milk has a zing."

That just popped out. Is Miki's talking style affecting me? Being so susceptible to Twain's and Bierce's quips, I must not let Miki enter my mind. Think obliquely, like Penrod! He's author Booth Tarkinngton's gifted 12-year-old who has verbal tricks so slick that he can twist life's spins into grins. I try to identify with him, although lacking an audience, apart from menehune.

I thank Ah Soong profusely. He bows and returns to the grotto; the two younger menehune quickly clear the area where I ate, then follow him.

Kahu explains: "Ah Soong once cooked for a band of Chinese pixies. They cut his Achilles tendons so he couldn't run away. That explains his walk. Waiting for a chance to escape, Ah Soong climbed onto a rickshaw and rode to Macao's harbor, where he joined your ancestor Chun Hung, who could see him as well as you can.

"King Kamehameha III, known as Kauikeaouli, initiated land reforms and allowed Chun Hung to initiate commercial sugar production in Hawai'i with the king as his partner. Chun Hung raised sugar and processed it in a mill on Maui. He sold his own brown and white granulated sugar in Hungtai, his Maui and Honolulu retail stores.

"Ah Soong, tireless worker, was Chun Hung's unseen right-hand man in the sugar mill, the store, and in his Pagoda Hotel. The hotel was famous for extraordinary food; Ah Soong concocted its fancy recipes.

When Kahu and I return to the clothesline, he confides, "Ah Soong, Miki, Rising Sun, other menehune, and I are unnoticed in the human world. We watch and hear what goes on. Being invisible, Big Persons don't know we're present and, of course, don't realize what we know.

"You see and communicate with little people. This is a very special gift. Keep it secret among us."

"Yes, I promise. I'll keep my secret journal, though." Kahu nods and disappears.

That night I read "Japan Reverts to Warfare" in H. G. Well's book, *The Shape of Things to Come.* He describes effects of a destructive and indecisive naval war in the western Pacific between Japan and the United States that never ends:

> The world slid back to political and social chaos.
> It was like the dreary and futile wars that effaced
> Asia Minor from history by the sponge of Islam.

The military government manages Hawai'i's news, allowing local newspapers to report, "By not being in Pearl Harbor the *Enterprise, Lexington,* and *Saratoga*—carriers of the core of the U.S. Pacific Fleet's airpower—escaped destruction on December 7."

I stop at the post office for the newspaper and mail on my way home from school. Several residents are chatting on its porch today about the strange situation involving

America's aircraft carriers that didn't show up at Pearl and have disappeared. Everyone agrees, "Japanese occupation is imminent."

Mother won't return from Hilo until tomorrow. I want company and go to the eucalyptus tree. Maybe Kahu will tell me more about the fighting we saw on the Kāne'ohe plains.

I prefer knowing about past battles instead of worrying about the ones to come.

8. Going Underground

Kahu gestures as I walk to the eucalyptus tree. I follow him through the rain forest onto Menehune Plains.

Seeing me look longingly at a hanging pomelo, Kahu says, "Pick and eat one and wait here until I call for you." He goes to the grotto, standing reflectively at its entrance. A subdued Miki steps out. They converse quietly together.

I've acquired the habit of processing information when nothing is going on and do so, while chewing slices of fruit with juice squirting over my chin. Kahu is tolerant about my head being in the clouds. He'll grunt or start talking to regain my attention.

I think about the battle on the Kāneʻohe plains. Not owning a watch, I've no idea of how long we watched; when we returned, the sun seemed in the same position as when we left. Apparently the world stands still while I travel with Kahu. With the help of an Episcopal rector, I am learning about things stated in The Bible being interpreted by poets—"The Bible is a book containing inspiration," he explains. For instance:

The time lapse I experiencd on the plains is similar to a verse in Psalm 90, a prayer of Moses:

> For a thousand years in your sight
> Are like a day that has just gone by.

That same thought, expressed by Issac Watts in 1719, is scored into the hymn, "Oh God Our Help in Ages Past," to music known as "Saint Ann." Coincidentally, that was last Sunday's sermon hymn in Kealakekua's Christ Church Episcopal. We did a unison reading of Psalm 90 that still echoes in my ears: "By thy wrath are we troubled. For all our days are passed away in thy wrath: we spend our years as a tale that is told."

The Rev. Kenneth O. Miller told us, "Although time seems to stand still during wartime uncertainties, we should anticipate a brighter side." He referenced Mathew Arnold's melancholy poem, "Dover Beach," and finished optimistically, for contrast, with words from a popular song expressing empathy for the brave English people:

> There'll be blue birds over
> The white cliffs of Dover,
> Tomorrow, just you wait and see.
> There'll be love and laughter
> And peace ever after
> Tomorrow, when the world is free.

I remember his sermons and what is associated with them because the Rev. Miller is teaching me to realize how a church service is structured. On Friday he previews what he will preach; Sunday I hear the real thing; then the following Tuesday, he asks me to review last Sunday's sermon.

He wants me to describe how "music and readings" relate. Repetition—three experiences to discuss content—causes details to stick in my head. That's his plan.

The Rev. Miller is preparing me for confirmation. After school, twice a week, I go to the parsonage to study the Bible and *The Book of Common Prayer* and for previews and reviews.

Mrs. Miller gives me homemade cookies and milk, which now I can drink because *my asthma seems gone!*

Kahu's eyes have stopped squinting; he's made up his mind and gestures and grunts. *He is going to take me inside there!* Just before the entry, there is a torch, and a pretty young menehune lady holds a spear near it.

"The sentinel means *Queen Esther is in,*" Kahu says cryptically.

I've heard about lava tubes.

Mother traveled through a lava tube in Kona with Bishop Museum scientists. She put photographs and typed explanations of the trip in an album. I remember her writing: "Lava leaves the eruption point in channels; tubes are conduits through which it travels beneath the surface. Surrounding lava develops walls as it cools, while the channel melts its way deeper. When the flow ceases, a long, cave-like tube remains."

Lava tubes can be extremely long. The tube Mother explored was from an 1859 flow. Lava entered the ocean *over thirty miles* from its eruption point.

She said Hawaiian families hid in tubes during wars. They sometimes used ledges as burial places. "Did you see bones in the tube?" I asked.

"Yes."

"Was there other stuff?"

She answered, "I was with Hawaiians. They wouldn't touch ancestral belongings and wanted to leave immediately. Scientists told us they would be exploring the tube to study its size."

Bones made Mother realize they shouldn't be in there.

The entranceway to this lava tube is about the size of our kitchen, which is three times bigger than my little clothes closet. We follow a left turn into a passage and walk downhill. Menehune are cracking *kukui* nuts and threading them onto sticks.

"They're making Hawaiian candles," Kahu explained. Aha! I realize: It's how the tube is lighted.

Little workers are as busy as Santa Claus' elves: weaving mats, carving bowls, making fishhooks. Some look up and smile tentatively.

We're about to make another turn when an intriguing aroma reaches us. "Where's that's fragrance coming from?"

"Queen Esther's lair," Kahu answers.

Miki grins, his eyes twinkling. Posturing, he places his left hand on his waist, elbow sticking out. He puts his right hand over his heart; slowly and dramatically, he extends it as he recites:

> Olfactory genius who persuades
> And any hesitation dissuades:
> Using blossom scents to create an urge

More fervent than by appearance or word.
Thrilling mixtures for sensitive noses:
Orange blossoms, lime, attars of roses,
Liliko'i, plumeria from our soil
Blended with almond and jojoba oil.
Clove, jasmine, bergamot, rosemary, musks,
Mokihana and gardenia are musts,
Tuberose, jasmine, *maile* to savor,
With rich ginger and coconut flavor.

Grinning, he waves both hands, pretending to waft aromas.

Queen Esther's Lair

9. Persian Storyteller

Kahu leads us around the turn into a large, decorated chamber. Finely woven *hala* mats are on its floor; bark cloth, dyed into patterns of differing brown shades, hang from the wall; gourds filled with flowers are scattered around the area.

About a dozen beautiful young menehune ladies sit and lie on the mats; others stand around the chamber. They wear colorful patterns of cloth muumuu, a loose-fitting dress. One especially striking lady, a little taller than I, sits on a high-backed throne of woven pandanus leaves; her vivid silk gown clings to her body contours.

Aromas in the room cloud my senses. My pulse is racing.

I study Queen Esther.

Her shiny black hair flows across her forehead; the rest of her intricately woven hair reaches below her shoulders. I absorb what I see: eyelids shaded with bright turquoise, radiant blue eyes rimmed with black liner, painted eyebrows creating a quizzical expression, rouged high cheeks, smiling full and shiny bright red lips, brilliant-white teeth.

Mirror, mirror on the wall, Queen Esther is indeed the fairest of all—pretty German brunette Snow White would seem plain by contrast.

She is slim, but—as Jack London described his ladies—"very buxom." Queen Esther wears a crimson gown, she's adorned with a bright blue stone necklace, and she has gold bracelets on both arms. When she extends her right hand in my direction, I see a rainbow array of rings on her fingers.

The aroma wafting from her hand isn't heavy or cloying—it's just *there!*

I feel giddy.

"Good afternoon, Queen Esther," Kahu says, slowing using the lower range of his rich voice and lowering his head. "This is Arthur. We've just observed one of Palei'oholani's battles."

Am I supposed to genuflect?

She speaks. Maybe she sings. I've read descriptions of a Stradivarius violin played by a maestro. It's how her voice sounds. I tingle as she begins, and I am quivering when she ends.

"Please call me Esther. I am pleased to see you, having heard about you."

"Yes ma'am, thank you."

"So you have been introduced to old Hawaiian warfare. Remember it when you read Homer. *The Iliad* will give you insight on ancient warfare—ceremony, bravado, and warrior psyche. All relates to what you saw today."

She raises her left arm, making a sweeping gesture. She wears sparkling rings on that hand as well.

"Hawaiians are splendid on the battlefield. Using sticks and stones, they demonstrate heroic valor. Going to war with reckless courage, professing to fear nothing— *Kahuna* stimulate them by saying death is not an end of life, but a passage to another . . . to a superior existence— to their Valhalla. Do you understand what that is?"

"Yes. Siegfried is there." She smiles.

Shouldn't I address her as "Queen Esther?" I will. When uneasy, I revert to "my hesitant being-screened-for-a-foster-home" behavior. I wait for her to continue.

"Kahu speaks of you as 'cerebral.' He didn't say you're tongue-tied."

It's true, I feel knotted up. "Yes, ma'am." Interrogation makes my voice quaver.

The maidens titter. Esther stretches both arms, wafting another wave of exquisite aromas. She gives a big, leisurely smile, stretches her shoulders, then sighs—apparently for no reason.

"Please sit down. I'll tell you about me before meeting your ancestor Kualiʻi.

"This is about life in Persia—now known as Iran— over fourteen hundred years ago, when it was ruled by Xerxes.

"All that Old World grandeur came to naught. A Latin summary: 'Sic transit Gloria mundi'—'Thus passes the glory of the world.' Only ruins remain of Xerxes' capital."

Kahu nods wisely. Miki, looking as if he would like to say something, hesitates to interrupt.

She lowers the palm of her hand; I sit, and so do all the young women. They look attentively at Queen Esther. Perched on a little rise at the back of the tube, Miki and Kahu cross their legs and give her their complete attention.

"In Hebrew, my name means 'Morning Star,'" she begins. "My family was deported from Jerusalem to Babylon in 599 B.C. After my parents died, Mordecai, father's brother, brought me to Susa, Persia's capital.

In 486 B.C., Xerxes inherited his kingdom from Darius, his father, who was known as 'The King of Kings'—Lord of Asia, Master of Africa, and a major force in Europe as well.

"King Xerxes expanded the kingdom, amassing huge revenue in the form of tribute—yearly taxes from subjugated countries.

"His elite troops, called 'The Immortals,' methodically overran Greece. A rebellion broke out in Egypt and Babylonia, prompted by Xerxes' increasing their tax levies to finance continual conquests. Xerxes put down the rebellion and demolished Babylon, which once was Persia's capital city; as an insult, he commanded Babylon yearly to send him five hundred castrated young men as servants.

"Celebrating the rebellion's end, King Xerxes held a 180-day feast in Susa. At one point, he ordered his queen, Vashti, to wear her crown and appear naked before him and his guests, so he could show everyone how beautiful she was. She was having a party of her own in the harem and refused to obey that humiliating order.

"A nasty man named Haman, one of the king's advisors, teased the king: 'If word gets around, no one's wife will think she has to listen to her husband.' Guests snickered. At Haman's urging, Xerxes ordered Vashti put to death!

"Wanting the formality of having a queen, King Xerxes initiated a search throughout the kingdom for another beautiful young woman.

"Tribute Day, the first of April, was one of the few occasions the public saw their king. Uncle normally kept me secluded, but this year's was an important event as it marked Xerxes' twentieth ruling year. Uncle Mordecai took me to it.

"Thousands of spectators were held back from the broad avenue by a line of warriors in dress uniforms. The crowd let loose a loud roar as his majesty emerged from the Apadana—the great audience hall. Xerxes sat on a golden throne mounted on a platform; a tasseled red canopy swayed above his head with the measured step of the throne bearers—a squad of The Immortals chosen from among his most imposing-looking warriors. They strode proudly.

"Xerxes wore a crimson robe and gold crown. The canopy was embroidered with lions, bulls, and the winged symbol of his god Ahuramazda—on whom Zoroaster based his new religion in about 600 B.C."

I am actually following this ancient history. Ten-cent comic books carry full-page ads about an ancient prophet named Zoroaster whose predictions, made in 600 B.C., *are happening right now*—the ads state! I buy War Stamps instead of comic books and pay for them by collecting empty soda water bottles and turning them in for grocery store refunds. Mother thinks I'm quite enterprising. Once you fill a book with $18.75 in War Stamps, you can give it to the post office for a War Bond worth $25 after ten years—if we win the war.

Whoops! Wandering mind—will Queen Esther notice? Studying me, she says something about which I have absolutely no connection.

"Zoroaster introduced the idea of an afterlife offering reward or punishment, depending on one's lifetime decorum. Jews hadn't considered that."

She continues describing Tribute Day. I must concentrate on what she says so she won't stare at me again.

"The king maintained a regal pose as soldiers lowered him to the ground. Then he nodded his head, a signal to continue with the program.

"Over a hundred guardsmen, the first marchers, were dressed in intricately patterned gowns of yellow, turquoise blue, white, and brown. Then came grooms with horses from the royal stable and two empty chariots—one, symbolically, for the king and one for the deity Ahuramazda.

"Next were lords of the realm who didn't march but walked with gravity. Each Persian wore a flower gown and fluted felt tiara. Medes were dressed in leather trousers, tunics, laced shoes, domed felt hats, and sleeved overcoats worn cape-fashion over their shoulders. Nobles of both nations had on lots of gold—earrings, bracelets, heavy neck rings. These glittered in the sunlight as they walked. Dignitaries passed by, paying homage to the king. Then the tribute procession began. A Persian usher clasped the leader of each national group to guide him along.

"On and on they came: Dozens of men from India carried a pair of vases in baskets suspended by a yoke. Gasps came from the crowd, knowing the vases contained pure gold dust.

"Representatives of all nations passed by with wagons full of embroidered clothing, honey-rich beehives, and fine wrought weapons.

"Five hundred young eunuchs, Babylon's enforced tribute, walked with downcast eyes.

"**I** was spotted by two of the king's guards. They approached my uncle and inquired about me. He didn't let on that we are Jewish. They took me with them, and my life changed immediately.

"I was entrusted to Hegai, the eunuch in charge of the harem, and won his favor. He selected maids from the king's palace to serve me and moved us into the very best place within the large building housing the harem.

"The royal harem was a sizeable community of the realm's most attractive women.

"Before a girl's turn came up to go to King Xerxes, she had to complete twelve months of prescribed beauty treatments: six months with oil of myrrh and six with perfume and cosmetics. I became extremely interested in making perfumes and other intriguing potions. It became my specialty." Scents within the lava tube demonstrate her proficiency.

"When the time came, the chief concubine took the chosen virgin to the king's palace in the evening. In the morning she was not allowed in the harem but became other officials' concubine. After one night with the king, she was palace chattel.

"Evidently I was just what Xerxes wanted. He married me after our night together and I became known as 'Queen Esther.'

"Uncle Mordecai told me to continue hiding my faith from the king and his advisors.

"Our intrigue worked well. King Xerxes didn't throw any elaborate parties in which I had to display myself in the buff. He had harem visitors. Uncle stuck to his rigid form of Judaism and I enjoyed being with the girls."

Esther stops, studying my face for reactions.

I enjoy how she tells the story. Her "Stradivarius voice" varies in tempos and tones, skipping along with a staccato pace and leisurely drawing out long passages. It is exquisite. I would be enthralled if she spoke in Hebrew.

The scent of ginger is behind me. I turn, and a smiling young menehune lady hands me a coconut shell cup filled with a beverage. I thank her and sip the lime drink.

One of the ladies presents a cup to Esther. Miki coughs and sputters. A court member walks over, hands him a cup of juice, and he grins smugly.

Queen Esther pauses before resuming her story.

This is like grand opera.

Uncle Buster Cook in Hilo encourages my listening to the Metropolitan Opera Saturday broadcasts. This started after I told him about Daddy Holzclaw. We sat on his patio and heard *Samson and Delilah* by Charles Camille Saint-Saens. Delilah's siren song, "Mon couer s'ouvre a ta voix," captivated me—as it did Samson. Milton Cross interprets operas for the radio audience, but he didn't explain the words of the song in Buster's florid detail. He said a sweet voice can open a heart and make a smitten man mindless. Queen Esther is creating new emotions within little puppy me.

Smiling, she picks up the story.

"When Haman became prime minister of Persia, he thought everyone should bow down to him. Uncle Mordecai, the gatekeeper, refused. This made Haman furious! Being a gatekeeper was a very prestigious position. Uncle Mordecai didn't have to kowtow to officials.

"Those seeking an audience with the king passed into the gatehouse, which was under my uncle's supervision. It was a large hall, eighty feet square and sixty feet high, with tall columns at the top of which were massive sculptures of paired bulls, lions, and monsters. The grandeur inspired awe.

"Visitors remained there until summoned to the Apadana—the audience hall, which was a separate building beyond the gatehouse. Gatekeeper Mordecai helped to prepare visitors for the majesty within the palace audience hall.

"When an announcement was made that the monarch was ready, dignitaries entered the hall and approached the empty throne. Inscribed on the stone stairways of the audience hall were the words, 'I am the Great King in this great earth far and wide.' After an interval, the king ceremoniously entered by a side door to greet his guests.

"Uncle Mordecai was responsible also for the care and display of palace treasure. He inventoried everything and served as the king's museum keeper.

"That huge complex was filled with tribute. Chambers in the building were crowded with gold- and silver-plated furniture, exquisitely fashioned bowls, plates, vases, and drinking vessels of gold, silver, alabaster, crystal, and costly Egyptian glass.

"Its rooms contained sumptuous Persian carpets, ceremonial gold armor and weapons, ivory and pearls, jewelry, precious stones, frankincense, rare spices, and bolts of fabulous silk, much of it dyed with the distinctive Tyrian purple reserved for royalty. Ingots of gold lay about the treasury's working areas.

"Haman hated Jews. He decreed that in Adar of the coming year, on the thirteenth day of the month, all Jews were to be killed. None could leave. There would be no place to hide from the murderers.

"Uncle Mordecai sent me a message about Haman's plot, asking me to go to the king on Jews' behalf.

"I hadn't seen the king for a month. No one could without being invited. Mustering up my courage, I visited Xerxes, who acted angry over my imposition. But I quickly calmed him down.

"Later, as we drank wine, Xerxes asked, 'Now, what is your request? Even up to half the kingdom, it will be granted.'

"I *really* knew how to manage that man. I asked to have Haman join us for dinner the next night.

"Haman felt puffed up over being asked to dine with the king and queen. Only on a public holiday did the king dine in the presence of his courtiers. At other times he ate alone, separated from his guests by curtains. This was tantamount to declaring a holiday in Haman's honor! Or so Haman thought.

"Strutting around, Haman became furious that gatekeeper Mordecai refused to bow to him. He decided to have a gallows built where he'd have Uncle Mordecai hung.

"Unable to sleep, the king ordered the record of his reign to be brought in and read to him. In anticipation, I'd asked Hegai to have the book turned to the page describing how Mordecai exposed a plot to assassinate King Xerxes.

"When reminded of this tale, the king asked the reader, one of Hegai's friends from Babylon, what reward Mordecai had received for this service. He said that nothing had been done for Mordecai.

"One of the king's attendants then told the king of the gallows Haman had built to hang Mordecai. Furious, the king ordered that Haman himself be hanged immediately on that new gallows!

"So Haman was hanging instead of dining."

Queen Esther pauses and smiles smugly. Every one of the young women beams but says nothing—the story is not over. "Morning Star" continues.

"I persuaded Xerxes to give Mordecai his signet ring and the right to save the Jews. Mordecai sent letters, bearing the mark from the king's ring pressed in wax, to all governors of Persia authorizing Jews to defend themselves. Jews took a bloody revenge on their enemies!

"This established an annual feast, the Feast of Purim, in memory of their deliverance.

"Xerxes no longer waged war. He and I enjoyed our cordial entente—my life in the harem and his life with young ladies trained by me. The king was so pleased with their deportment that he allowed them to return to the harem and to come see him again.

"I appeared on the throne with Xerxes and whispered enticing ideas during official ceremonies. It took his mind away from stuffy court matters."

The girls giggle.

I don't understand her French, but "cordial" sounds pleasant. The only marriage role models I've observed are elderly people who generally ignore each other.

Esther brings her Persian kingdom story to a quick conclusion.

"After a number of years of staying off the battlefield and dipping and redipping into the harem, King Xerxes was stabbed to death by a subordinate who was angry the Persian Empire wasn't expanding.

"I moved to rebuilt Babylon for a while, then headed to the rebuilt city of Athens. I'd acquired the power of everlasting life and beauty, with the help of my young ladies. No one would believe who I'd been. I had no difficulties finding an amusing social life."

Losing her dreamy look, Esther turns businesslike.

"Jews' battles of revenge began on the thirteenth of Adar. The Jewish calendar shows that commemorative date is coming up in two weeks.

"Arthur, will you find out when the welfare commodity truck's delivery completes its monthly deliveries? Does your mother have leftover sugar and flour?"

I nod. "Lots of extra bags from last month are in the old hospital operating room."

"Good—we'll use it for our Purim celebration. Does your mother have baking pans?"

I nod again: "In our basement."

"Very fine. Then I will talk with you tomorrow; you can help with the arrangements. Good-bye."

She looks away to devote attention to the young women closest to her.

I stand in front of Queen Esther, bow, and then leave. I would've clicked my heels first—it's what Dorothy did in Oz—I read somewhere it's a court custom. But I'm barefoot—don't own shoes.

I join Kahu and Miki at the back of the chamber. We walk to the grotto entrance.

Once there, Miki says, "Bye, you made a nice try," then strolls away. Kahu moves his head in the direction of the trail. I follow him down the hill.

At the eucalyptus tree he says, "Queen Esther likes you. I'd not heard that story. She talks about coming from America to Hawai'i with your ancestor or reminisces about dryad friends in the sandalwood forests. She shares very little of herself, actually; she just asks questions and appears wise—private and queenly.

"Can you be here tomorrow?" Kahu asks. "We'll go to see Kuali'i."

"Tomorrow is Thursday? Yes, Monday, Wednesday, and Thursday are free for me. I go to the Reverend Miller's home Tuesday and Friday afternoons."

"Please be here after school," Kahu replies and vanishes.

10. Disguised Warrior

At our rendezvous point the next day, I find a big, rosy mango sitting on a ti leaf under the tree. Juice is dripping down my chin when Kahu appears. He smiles at how eagerly I eat the sweet and tangy fruit.

"Take your time, then we'll travel. Miki wants to come."

Sure enough, he steps out from the bushes, smiling as usual. Watching me finish slurping, Miki hands me his handkerchief and advises:

> Irish linen: wipe the goo off your chin,
> That mango's from Kaua'i, it's a Haden.

Sensing my hesitancy, Kahu says, "Use the handkerchief.

"We are going to see your ancestor Kuali'i, a celebrated chief noted for strength and bravery. He had a great desire for war and won every battle he fought.

"It was customary for Kuali'i to accompany his soldiers into battles. But as they became more and more proficient, he let them go to war by themselves, staying behind at his home in Kailua on Oʻahu—so they thought. Soldiers usually told him the time and place the battles were to be fought to keep the king informed.

"Kualiʻi went to the battles as a disguised warrior, not wearing his regalia and without his soldiers' knowledge. He was there in the thick of it every time an engagement occurred. At the close of a battle, his men saw someone ahead of them come out of the conflict carrying an enemy chief's feather cloak. He disappeared on the way to Kailua."

Finishing the mango, I throw its seed in the bushes. Maybe it'll grow.

"Leave the handkerchief here," Kahu says. "We'll give it to one of Esther's young ladies to wash when we return.

"Kualiʻi left Oʻahu from Kailua and arrived on Kauaʻi at Kahaluʻu today. A boy saw him there this morning. Let's go."

Then Kahu tells me, "You didn't eat an ordinary mango. We enhanced it. You are as invisible as Miki and I. Only menehune can see you. You can be close enough to hear what people in the past say."

"I don't understand Hawaiian very well, especially the old version."

"You will. I made it possible. You'll also be able to read thoughts."

I'm accustomed to becoming involved in a book's drama. Kahu's given me power to climb inside minds before things play out.

I am eager to apply enhanced senses. Kahu touches my back, and instantly we're on a beach.

"This is Kauaʻi," he explains.

An old woman and a teenager are talking in front of a grass shack. I approach and listen.

"Tutu, that man runs so swiftly along the sea," says the boy.

"Watch him closely, Kekuni, I think he is King Kuali'i."

"When he reaches us, I'll follow him."

"Then carry this ti leaf packet—it contains shrimps. Take this fan left by his canoe, the king may need it. Now listen carefully: If the king looks behind him, sees the fan, and wants to know who you are, tell him. But don't go near him; avoid having your shadow pass over the king. Stay away from his lee side to avoid stepping over his shadow. Keep some distance away. Offer him the shrimp."

Kuali'i passes by. The boy stands up and follows. Kuali'i continues running, seeing the boy as he goes up a rise.

I don't want him following me, the king thinks. *No one should know my plans of going to battle.*

He runs faster, expecting to outrun the boy on Kahana sands.

I would've dropped out from exhaustion if Kahu hadn't bestowed the power for me to move effortlessly on a cushion of air.

Kuali'i sprints as he runs along the sea. Kekuni stays close behind. I understand the king's thoughts: *This boy's a fast runner!*

Kuali'i continues running to Waimea. There he sits by the side of the stream.

Kekuni wants to be near the king but stays on the other side. The sun has risen to its peak. He moves back, afraid his shadow might pass over Kualiʻi. Death is the penalty for violating this *kapu*.

Kualiʻi sees the boy keeping the fan by his side. *Will he use it?* Kekuni doesn't, because it's the king's. Kualiʻi would kill Kekuni if he shaded himself with the fan. That would violate a *kapu* about using things belonging to royalty.

After waiting for a while, Kualiʻi calls out to ask, "Who gave you that fan?"

"One of your honored servants," replies Kekuni.

"Where are you going?"

"I am following the king," the boy answers.

"If I should run and grab hold of a feather cloak, would you grab one too?"

"Yes I would."

"If I should seize hold of a man, would you seize one too?"

"Yes, I would," Kekuni responds, then asks, "Would you like these shrimp?" He moves forward to place them on a stone.

The king enjoys them.

They resume running. As afternoon shadows grow longer, Kekuni increases his distance behind the king.

Arriving in Līhuʻe, Kualiʻi learns that the two armies are encamped. He continues to the Kukaniʻoko battlefield.

Kualiʻi enters into the thickest part of the fight. Using his club, he breaks through the opposing army. The boy follows closely.

He heads to Pāʻia, where another battle is underway. Seeing the opposing king wearing a long feather cloak,

Kuali'i draws close, kills him, seizes the cloak, and walks away.

Kekuni cuts off one of the dead king's small fingers and one of his ears.

Kuali'i leaves the battlefield believing he is rid of the boy, who'll be unable to escape the melee. Looking behind, he sees Kekuni.

The boy catches up and asks the king, "How are you?"

"Just as usual," replies Kuali'i.

He says to Kekuni, "Where is your man?"

"When you took the feather cloak, I took a small finger and one of his ears."

His answer makes Kuali'i decide, *This is a brave lad!*

They resume their journey until reaching where the king's canoe has been pulled up near a cove. The king asks his waiting servant for an extra *malo* (loincloth). Kuali'i fastens it on the boy. By doing so, he bestows royal recognition and reward for faithful service.

Mind reading is fun.

K ahu walks over: "It'll be some time before Kuali'i's canoe reaches O'ahu. Let's talk with Esther about her party, then we'll see the end of this episode."

He touches my back. The three of us are at Menehune Plains; one of Ah Soong's helpers scoots forward.

"Inform Esther we are here," Kahu says.

This gathering is less staged than our first, and only two young women are with her.

I assure Esther that enough leftover sugar and flour is stored in the unlocked operating building. "I will find the baking pans so whoever you send won't make a clamor hunting for them at night and cause my mother to investigate what's happening."

Seeing pots and pans moving around on their own in the hands of an invisible menehune might unnerve her. She's smoking lots of Lucky Strike cigarettes "because of job pressures," she says.

I tell Queen Esther, "Kahu has promised I'll learn more about the legend of Kuali'i."

She nods. "Good. When you come back, I can tell you about your ancestor's journey to America. It's why I am here."

I step back several paces. Having watched Kekuni, I'll make certain that my shadow, lit by *kukui* candles, does not fall on Queen Esther.

While following Kahu through the tunnel, I greet the busy craftsmen, who wave back. At the front of the grotto, Kahu applies his magic touch.

We arrive at Kailua, O'ahu. Kuali'i, his men, and Kekuni are pulling their canoe out of the water. I notice how Kekuni avoids letting his or Kuali'i's shadows cross.

I follow Kuali'i and Kekuni as they walk into a settlement. Kuali'i tells Kekuni to wait as they approach the houses. "You stay here while I go on ahead to the *mua*. This is the men's eating house. When you hear the beating of the drum, someone will come for you."

Kuali'i strides forward. Shortly after, a drum begins to beat and a man steps out from the *mua* and beckons to Kekuni.

Walking up to lead me away, Miki quietly says:

There are rituals at ceremonies—
'Tis better if they remain mysteries.
Kahuna are like our Celtic Druids—
They use horror to create memories.

How'd Miki know that I knew about Druids?

It's hands-on-my-back time again by Kahu. At the tree, after promising to be here tomorrow, I say to Kahu, "May I ask you something?"

"Yes."

"You doctored up that mango to make me invisible. Will my mother know I'm in the room?"

"Kneel slightly." He touches my forehead.

"Now she will."

I enter our basement and pull out baking pans and cookie sheets to place them on a worktable. Mother is away. I reflect on being invisible and reading minds in the sixteenth century.

My mind is whirling. I hope Kekuni's celebration went okay. He was very careful. I didn't see him touch the king's shadow. Maybe I will learn more about Druids from Miki. Then I'll tell him of my own experience with Sir Galahad in Kaimuki. I feel very tired—wonder what that mango was laced with? *Zzz.*

11. Battle of Chicanery

Each rendezvous with my menehune mentor usually begins with my climbing the eucalyptus tree and Kahu then appearing. Sometimes he's waiting under the tree.

He pops out from the bushes today.

"Hi, Kahu. Thank you for yesterday's interesting trip. Did you bring a mango? Where's Miki?"

"Mango's not needed today," he replies. I've a spell to cloud you from sight; you won't be close enough to hear what's happening on the big field. I'll explain the drama. No mind reading will be needed. Miki has been working on something to explain to you."

I see rustling in the undergrowth and hear:

> Grr-reetings R-rath! I'm ready to dance a ring.
> 'One for all and all for one,' we will sing!

Miki emerges; Kona's Three Musketeers are ready for adventure. I turn, Kahu touches my back, and away we go.

We are in another part of Waiʻanae, looking down on a plain similar to the one where Oʻahu-Kauaʻi forces defeated Hawaiʻi's invading army. Only one army is on it.

Miki stands in front of us. He seems very proud, as if having something important to say. Kahu explains: "Miki wants to introduce what we'll witness. Here's some background before he begins.

"That army below is comprised of warriors who fight for the chief from Koʻolauloa. It is 1775; your ancestor Kualiʻi—who yesterday you saw as a young man running on a beach—is now 170 years old. He is bent with age, withered, his eyes are reddened, and he is carried around in netting."

Kahu points: "You will see him in the net up there on the hill. He still goes to battle, but now as a spectator. Sit down, make yourself comfortable."

Turning his head, he gestures: "Miki, your turn."

Standing with his hands folded in front of him and a serious expression on his face, the leprechaun declares:

> Composer-performers will now grow rich,
> The first Rock-Age Concert they plan to pitch.
> Two brothers came up with this bold new scheme
> To start and win a war without fighting.
> Hawaiians, wishing to market a chant,
> Selected the biggest king's name to rant.
> One tells a chief, "War will bring you fame:
> Go after the big guy on your home plain."
> Chief asks of his priest—it's part of gaming:
> "A sign, 'Oh Gods—Winning or Defaming.'"
> "His army's too huge, no chance," says the priest.
> "Victory's destined, your fame will not cease"
> Are beguiling words from second brother:

"We'll reach the field first before the other,
"Once in position, your army will win:
A sure thing. You'll knock them out on the chin."
Brother One gets a bribe to set things up,
The dupe's soldiers on Ewa's Plains then sup.
Brothers have signals ready for patsies—
War initiators being nasties!
On Ewa's Plains are soldiers twelve hundred,
Around them are men twelve thousand numbered.
"I'll kill you Brother One, we're surrounded!"
"Whoa! My chant will make all be dumbfounded.
"Just listen, you'll go home safely and proud.
Step back, Chief, my voice will be very loud."
Brother Two stands near the chief on the hill,
Looks down at Brother One "Among the swill—
"Refuse, scraps, death" taunts the large army's men—
Who're silenced by words rising up to them:
"O Kuali'i, the axe with heavenly edge!
Following is the train of clouds after Kuali'i!
Drawn down is the horizon by Kuali'i."
To Kuali'i that sounded real good.
A chief says, "Why delay, fight now we should."
"The king's name is mentioned, we must hear more,"
Says Brother Two holding open the door:
"If he can name all your ancestors right,
Then why not call off this petty small fight?"
Brothers had written a script that was tight,
Their words would soothe anger, calming the might.
An eruption, once this line is ringing:
 "Stand forth at the call, and at the pleading."
The king stands; the whole army joins with him,
Brother One continues, wearing a grin.
The End: And two armies come together
Just handshakes, Rock-Age Concert is over.
The small army's chief turns over some land.

Unasked, Kaua'i's king yields his whole island.
Such is the value of well-written stuff,
Two Hawaiian boys pulled off one big bluff.
Brother One talks with the king that he saved:
"Wai'anae gave you safety, not a grave,
"You promised land before all that I said,
Why not make me your chief steward instead?"
Controlling storehouses proved a good deal,
Two sharing brothers—fealty and real.

I clap and grin. The leprechaun blushes, his rosy face almost matching the red hair peeking from under his hat brim.

"Miki covered the main points," Kahu says. Then he explains.

"The chant was a get-rich-quick scheme by two brothers who composed the *mele*. It was based on Kuali'i's legend, lineage, and accomplishments.

"Brother One urged Brother Two to visit Lonoikaika to talk him into going to battle—just as Miki described. Then devious Brother One told Kuali'i's war leader that Lonoikaika planned an insurrection, so let's creep up on them.

"Both armies are now here in O'ahu on 'Ewa's Plains." Kahu points: "You can see Kuali'i and his attendants there on top of the hill, but his twelve thousand warriors are staying out of sight behind the hill."

Lonoikaika's army has twelve hundred soldiers.

"Brother One put the knotted ti leaf on the pile of sugarcane peelings. You can see it down there on the edge of the field. That's the signal to Brother Two that Kuali'i's army has arrived and is staying out of sight beyond the ridge.

"Brother Two, pretending to be a priest, has convinced Lonokaika that he'll be victorious, because he won't be up against a formidable army. Brother Two was given land for such a favorable prediction."

I look down on the army of twelve hundred men, milling around, exercising, seemingly confident.

Then Kuali'i's army appears from behind the hill. The smaller army mills around in confusion, probably thinking of the trouble they are in. Some drop their spears, as if intending to sprint away.

"Look over there," Kahu tells me. "Priests thrust their arms furiously at Brother Two. They want him killed for his trickery."

"What's the king saying?"

"He is threatening to kill Brother Two and all his relations and all his friends.

"Kapa'ahulani, who is Brother Two, is asking the king for permission to chant his prayer. He explains that if his prayer is acceptable, they will all be saved. The king doesn't want to die and agrees.

"Now Brother Two is stepping toward where Kuali'i can look down and hear him chant the flattering *mele* the two brothers composed."

Not having eaten a mango, I can't hear or understand the chant. But I realize it is a panegyric—a formal speech of praise, as was "The Song of Roland" about a battle between the Spanish (Saracens) and Charlemagne's French (Franks) in 778—over nine hundred years before what I am now witnessing.

Something very dramatic is happening—Kuali'i's attendants are lifting him up while he is still in the netting.

Kahu says, "Kapaʻahulani has reached the exciting portion in his chant where it states, 'Stand forth at the call, at the pleading hold not a deaf ear.'

"As Kualiʻi is held upright, soldiers of the two wings of his army also stand and echo Kapaʻahulani's words; thousands of voices roar with fervor:

> *E ku mai oe i ka hea i ka uwalo,*
> *Mai hoʻokuli mai oe.*

As Kapaʻahulani is finishing, Kahu waves his hand. Magically, I understand what the crowd is shouting:

> The sun rises, it comes forth;
> By the power of the great-voiced Kualiʻi
> Was the sun given!

The two armies come together.

"They are exchanging *honi*. Kualiʻi has declared the battle is 'off,'" Kahu explains.

"The king of Koʻolauloa will yield the districts of Koʻolauloa, Koʻolaupoko, Waialua, and Waiʻanae to Kualiʻi. When the king of Kauaʻi hears how Kualiʻi gained the victory, he will offer Kualiʻi the island of Kauaʻi.

"By the event you have just witnessed, Kualiʻi gains supremacy over all the islands, although he does not stake his claim."

The leprechaun has a glazed expression. Kahu turns, smiles, and says, "I liked your chant and delivery, Miki."

Nodding in agreement, I don't feel Kahu touching my back.

12. Kuali'i Visits America

Back at the eucalyptus tree, Kahu motions for Miki and me to sit.

"Attah, you saw Kuali'i as an old man being carried in a *kōkō.* He kept his strength for a long time and lived until he was 175. When he was upwards of ninety years old, his son Pelei'oholani came from Kaua'i to visit him in Kailua. Maybe they drank too much *awa,* and a quarrel arose between them.

"Kuali'i was an expert at the art of *lua,* or *ku'ialua,* its formal name. Sometime I will take you to learn about it. But back to the quarrel.

"The son assaulted the father, and in the scuffle the old man placed a *lua* grip on Pelei'oholani. This gave Kuali'i complete mastery; he could've broken his son's bones in midair if he threw him.

"Instead, Kuali'i released Pelei'oholani, who left immediately for Kaua'i. He didn't revisit O'ahu until after his father's death at age 175.

"Kuali'i was a young man when Queen Esther met him in America.

"Kuali'i visited Kahiki, that foreign, mysterious land where the white man dwelt with his proud manners and his strange language. That land was shrouded in mists and fog and could be reached only after a long voyage. It bordered the Pacific—being the western coast of America. This is described in 'The Chant of Kuali'i' in history books."

Kahu recites some of it:

> O Kahiki, land of the far-reaching ocean …
> Within is the land, outside is the sun;
> Indistinct is the sun and the land when
> approaching …
> A land with a strange language is Kahiki …
> Kanakas, men of our race, are not in Kahiki,
> One kind of man is in Kahiki—the Haole white man.
> He is like a god …
> … Wandering about, and the only man who got
> there …
> Was Kuali'i indeed.

I am spellbound. My teacher continues the story as we walk through Shangri-la.

"Pacific islands were visited by Spanish navigators when Kuali'i was a boy. Passing Spanish galleons picked up Kuali'i and his company while they were fishing in O'ahu and carried them to the American coast—'The land within' as the chant says. Spaniards brought Kuali'i and his new companion back to Hawai'i on their return trip to the Philippines.

"Queen Esther will tell you more. Ready?"

I nod; we enter Menehune Plains. Outside the grotto, Kahu makes his bosun's whistle, and Rising Sun dashes out.

"Tell Queen Esther we're here."

The Japanese pixie scurries in; Kahu motions for me to sit. Ah Soong and a young assistant step out and hand us guava juice. We wait there until Rising Sun sticks his nodding head out from the grotto. We carry our coconut shell drinking cups in with us. Kahu, Miki, and I walk into the queen's aromatic lair.

Looking up, she says, "So you've heard of Kuali'i's trip to America?"

"Yes, but I don't understand why you left grand Persia for primitive America and then wanted to come to Hawai'i. Isn't that called 'wandering'?"

Esther raises and then drops her shoulders, releases a sharp breath, sits back in her woven chair, pauses, then answers, "I couldn't stay in any of those places; Our civilization was being destroyed.

"I'd left Persia because there's not much hometown hospitality for a murdered king's widow—particularly from his former foe. I traveled to Greece in the fifth century, enjoying the enlightened Athens during its golden age under Pericles, and I was in the company of great thinkers and societal critics—Socrates, Aristophanes, Plato, and Aristotle—'the Smarties.'

"Plato was extremely interested in Persian methods of education. He wrote of the conflict between good and evil, fundamental to the tenets of Zoroaster, and asked me in great detail about our court customs. During the fourth century B.C., Plato traveled extensively, going as far as Egypt. Wars prevented him from reaching Iran, which is what Persia is now called. I explained what I could, having been more interested in bodies than in minds during my harem times.

"Ironically, the name 'Iran' is related to the current war. Seven years ago when the Germans set out to change the world, their diplomats suggested that Persia be renamed Iran, which suggests Aryan roots, being a cognate of the word 'Aryan.'

"Back to 'the Smarties'; you'll eventually read their writings. I enjoyed Socrates' irony."

Raising her right arm, she shakes a finger at me: "Arthur, be wary of possible outcomes should you have too much to say. Some people don't appreciate wise guys. It's why Socrates had to drink hemlock and die."

She lowers her arm, opens her hands, places her chin within them, bends over, and leans forward. Her eyes are almost closed as she begins reminiscing in a slow, deep voice—as if her story is played solely on a Stradivarius violin's low G-string.

"I went to Rome, which was very social, if you were rich, attractive, everlastingly young, and didn't mention being Jewish. Rome became tedious after a few centuries; there were rumors the barbaric Celts and Huns might be coming—Oops, sorry, Miki! I looked for Israel's Lost Tribes, hearing rumors they planned another Exodus.

"Some groups of Jews had sailed from Jerusalem—to where, no one knew. I joined one large contingent with ships headed to the New World.

"New World colonists split into two large nations. I was among industrious Nephites, who raised herds of cattle and developed Old World crops such as wheat fields and barley. They were knowledgeable about iron, copper, brass, gold, and silver, which they found in America. They constructed a temple similar to Solomon's.

"Lamanites were in complete contrast—lazy, full of mischief, multiplying like rabbits, and barbaric. They dwelt in tents, roamed the wilderness, and hunted beasts of prey with their bows and arrows.

"Eventually they attacked and destroyed Nephite cities. It was similar to Rome when barbarians invaded. Miki, I acknowledge your sensitivity about feisty, fighting Irish."

She leans forward. "Celts had their turn on the world stage. After Cuchulan's exploits, Celtic warriors having potential for world conquest fell under the power of fairy women. They followed them to Apple-Land—Avalon— leaving their hot-tempered, intense fighting spirit behind, to spread like Irish mist where it will."

Miki nods solemnly; Queen Esther continues.

"I lived with the cultured Nephites, who were being annihilated by Lamanites. We fled to the western coast. That is where I met Kuali'i. He and his companions were brought to shore from a large Spanish sailing boat that was going to work its way up the coast.

"Kuali'i—such a big, beautiful man—told me wonderful stories about his islands. He described sweet-scented flowers when I mentioned being a perfume maker. He talked about Hawai'i's beautiful daughters when he learned I liked hearing this. He told me about playing with menehune when a boy, and that they built things for him when he became a man.

"The Spanish sailing boat returned after filling its water casks. Canoe makers in Kuali'i's company chose to stay to travel with Spanish sailors, who, in a smaller boat, were headed up a huge river gorge to see giant trees that grew there. We sailed back to Hawai'i without them.

Some of Kuali'i's people rowed out to the Spanish boat to retrieve us.

"Kuali'i took me to Kaua'i to meet menehune. I was very happy there. When I heard that dryads lived in Hawai'i's sandalwood forests, I decided *this was the island for me.* Things were wonderful, until Kamehameha brought white men and cannons and his new kind of war.

"Sometime you will hear about my revenge. Hawai'i was never the same after I expressed *my* wrath."

Queen Esther snickers, her eyes flashing quickly to see if I caught the wordplay.

"Well, 'Tongue-tied,' you know how to come here on your own. Be back for fun tonight when it is dark. Go to your basement first; we returned your mother's baking utensils but didn't know where to place them. Please take care of that."

I return through the forest all the way home; Miki's staying behind to help prepare for tonight's celebration.

13. Purim Party

Mother's in Hilo, school's in session, I'm home alone. She left me a note suggesting things to do before she returns in a couple of days. I put away the baking pans, spiffed up the wooden floors with a mop and pine oil cleaner, and defrosted the kerosene refrigerator.

I have no difficulty following the trail back up in the moonlight. *Kukui* candles light up Menehune Plains. A bonfire is burning behind a hill.

Perhaps one hundred excited menehune run around; many of them have faces painted to resemble clowns. Some wear leis, probably made by Queen Esther's courtiers. She walks up, nods, and points to menehune giggling and gobbling jelly-filled pastries. These are "Haman's Ears," one says, offering me one. Delicious!

I ask Queen Esther why they're called that.

"To recall how Haman's ears were his downfall for listening to those who suggested he use his position to bring about the destruction of the Jews. Menehune know only that they taste delicious—thanks to your mother's sugar, flour, jelly—and Ah Soong's marvelous baking skills. Here, have another."

"I don't see Miki."

"He's sprawled there." She points to him lying under tree ferns past the grotto.

"About a year ago, he and Ah Soong built a distillery and used ti-leaf roots to make *'ōkolehao*. After aging that high-proof spirit in a barrel, they poured it into empty Coca-Cola bottles and sealed the bottles with *kukui* nuts. They've been uncorking them, drinking *'ōkolehao*—I don't know if it's like whiskey or gin—but it made them jolly.

"Ah Soong's worked up enough courage to sing with Kahu over there. Miki's been happily entertaining himself. He had an audience for a while. But his repetitive 'arithmetic song' drove all away."

"Arithmetic?"

"Yes, he'd counted to almost 'a hundred bottles of booze on the wall'; by then everyone was gone."

"I'll go to see him."

His head on a log, Miki turns it to me with a happy grin. Empty bottles are scattered around him. "Gr-r-reetings, R-r-rath."

It sounds like his mouth is full of mush. *'Ōkole* is the part of your body you sit on, and *hao* (how) means "with force." He is "sloshed"—drinking it forcefully put him on his *'ōkole*. Miki hollers in a hoarse voice:

> This Revolutionary War song rings
> About three roguish chaps who could not sing.

He slurred every "s" in those lines; now he demonstrates his present inability to carry a tune:

> The first one was a baker,
> The second was a tailor.
> The third a candlestick maker . . .

Afraid the song includes many tedious verses, I interrupt. "Nice. It's enough, Miki."

Miki decides to try another one.

"Your grandmither" would love thith nith Scotch song—"

No she wouldn't—not from a singer in his lisping condition. Grandmother's of Scottish descent, but she had been an abolitionist before joining the Salvation Army. However, I nod courteously, willing to hear his tribute to dear ole Granny. He begins in his *ōkolehao* tenor:

> "Maxwelton's braes are bonnie
> Where early fa's the dew
> And 'twas there that Annie Laurie
> Gave me her promise true.
> Gave me her promise true
> Which ne'er forgot will be
> And for bonnie Annie Laurie
> I'd lay me doon and dee."

Not understanding "braes, fa, doon, and dee," I interrupt: "Have to go, Esther's beckoning."

I walk away as he repeats, "I'd lay me doon and dee."

Esther opens a ti-leaf packet and removes a lei woven of brown *haole koa* seeds interspersed with red *wiliwili* seeds—a very striking pattern. She says, "Jews give gifts today to people of whom they are fond. Bend your neck, Arthur."

I do, and she places the lei over my head. Scented like a gardenia, she kisses me, which is what you do when presenting a lei, and says, "Happy Purim."

Standing straight and proud, my face blushes while answering: "Thank you for making this day possible, Queen Esther. You were very brave."

She smiles and strolls away. I look at the back of her, noticing how vibrant the deep blue *holokū* looks: It is moving as if she's doing the hula.

Festooned with seeds, I saunter around, feeling special. No one pays attention; I'm a fixture now, and everyone's caught up in his or her activity.

Girls dance around a Maypole, twirling streams of ribbons. Groups of boys tumble—turning summersaults, performing cartwheels, doing "wheelbarrows"; one holds another's legs and wheels him along the ground on his hands. Kahu plays a ukulele; he and Ah Soong sing to a cluster of menehune girls. The Chinaman, always speaking in a singsong manner, is doing what for him is melodically natural.

Esther walks around sharing her scent.

Off to the corner, a gang plays "pee wee." This is like baseball, except that a stick instead of a ball is hit. One group stands in the field, another is at bat—meaning one person at a time takes a turn trying to hit the small stick the pitcher tosses toward him. If the batter misses the stick, he strikes out. Fielders try to catch a hit stick, then take three huge steps toward a slim crevice, a small slot dug in the ground where the batter is standing. If the stick is not caught, they throw it from where they pick it up at the slot.

The fielder's objective is to throw the stick so it touches the slot. The batter uses his larger stick, while bent over in a scooping motion, to fan away the thrown stick. If the small stick misses touching the slot, the batter can hit the smaller stick into the field. If not caught, he marks off the distance from the slot to where the stick lands. That distance is his score.

This is the way I interpret that game—is it menehune cricket? The next event has more action and is easier to follow.

Kahu whistles his bosun's call, everyone leaves the field, and several little folk carry away the Maypole.

Two teams of eight players line up facing each other on opposite sides of the field. Two fat menehune lug cardboard grocery store boxes to opposite ends of the field. They place the boxes about ten feet apart, marking the goal area. They will be goalkeepers.

Dressed in his white sailor suit and wearing a plumeria lei, Rising Sun marches to the center of the field. He carries a rubber ball I haven't seen for a long time, for it just disappeared. It's about six inches in diameter; I used to bounce and catch it off our water tank. A police whistle on a cord is around Rising Sun's neck—maybe from the Japanese ship that brought him to Hilo a decade ago.

Players wear baggy boxer shorts knotted around their waists. I guess Kahu is not the only menehune who robs clotheslines.

Referee Rising Sun blows the whistle to start the soccer ball game: It is Skins versus Shirts. Actually, it is Shreds of Shirts vs. Skins. Menehune on the Shirts team wear torn pieces of Aloha shirts in a variety of ways. Some have hats made of sleeves, others with headbands tied from ripped strips, and some have tied a piece of cloth band around their chest. It's a rag-tag team; many are wearing clown makeup.

Rising Sun blows the whistle a lot because menehune have merged soccer with football, making tackles and flying cross-body blocks. Skins win, 30 goals to 20. No one's injured badly, and players help each other hobble off the field.

Filled with Haman's ears, I go home with a sugar high and place the lei over my bedpost. It'll be the first thing I'll see tomorrow, Saturday morning.

Even though I'm ten and cavorting with spirits of which she wouldn't approve, I always say Grandma's bedtime prayer:

> No I lay me down to sleep,
> I pray the Lord my soul to keep:
> May God guard me through the night
> And wake me in the morning light.

During an opera broadcast, Uncle Buster and I heard Hansel and Gretel sing something similar to this as a lullaby when they were lost in the woods.

14. Kaua'i Menehune Valley

In the morning I lift the seed lei from my bedpost while climbing out of bed, putting it on for "dress up" should Kahu take me someplace today. Konawaena is on spring break. Easter Sunday is this weekend. Mother is staying with relatives in Kohala while working with clients there, and she won't be back until tomorrow.

While water on the kerosene stove heats for my tea and hot cereal, I take out a drawing pen and ink and open the cover of the *Oxford Book of Modern Verse, 1892–1935*. Aunt Eva sent it as an Easter gift, realizing my reading is not confined to children's literature.

I add more swirls to the elaborate calligraphy line border on the bookplate I've drawn of a fairy resembling Queen Esther, adding wings. She's in a garden peering out. Propping the cover open so the ink will dry, I head to the eucalyptus tree

Kahu pops from the guava bushes as soon as I am there. Some of the bushes shake and out stumbles bleary-eyed Miki. Kahu hands me a mango to chew and slurp so I'll understand what people we see say.

I ask, "Where are we going and when will it be?"

"To Kaua'i, and the time will be today, Thursday, April 20, 1942," he says, touching my back.

Instantly, we're at a high overlook. Kahu allows me a minute or so to catch my breath, for I'm awed by the grandeur. Then he says, in lecturing style, "This is called 'Nāpali'—'The Cliffs.' Trails of Kōke'e whisper secrets about flora, the fauna, even life itself. We're at Pihea Overlook—at 4,284 feet, these are the highest peaks overlooking Kaua'i's Nāpali Coast.

"To the north is Kalalau Valley. The steep-fluted ridges, red cliffs, waterfalls, and jungle extend 4,000 feet below us and run about a mile and a half to the ocean. To the south stretches the Alaka'i Swamp, source of Kaua'i's seven rivers. This is a forested plateau riven by deep, eroded, and unseen gorges and mountain summits hidden in eternal rainstorms."

What I am seeing is a grandiose painting brought to life—not of the Hudson River School, which I learned about in an art book, because of course, this is tropical. But the expanse, the feeling of majesty, the dark sense of mystery are similarly evocative.

Artists' imagery creates impressions that are becoming embedded in my impressionable young mind. Artists do for my psyche *exactly* what Ma Holzclaw said they would. You will meet her later.

Kahu points: "Mount Wai'ale'ale receives an average of 440 inches of rain a year. It is the wettest spot on earth." He is indoctrinating me intensively about this place that once was his home.

"We are here in spring 1942," he explains. "However, you will learn about how things were 1,500 years ago. That's when only menehune populated these islands."

Wisps of ragged clouds spiral in the valley below. They rise up toward the sun, revealing rainbows within their misty cores. Then turning silver and spectral, they cyclone over the ridge into the interior.

A sweet aroma rises to us. Is Esther here? I look to where Kahu points.

"The scent is from Oriental plum blossoms down there. Those trees are called *palama,* a Hawaiianized version of the English word 'plum.' Originally raised in China for thousands of years, they were imported to Japan about two hundred to four hundred years ago and circulated around the globe with the misnomer 'Japanese plum.' The official title is 'Methley.' It has red-purple skin and soft, juicy, sweet blood-red flesh.

"Your grandfather's brother supervised the planting of *palama* trees down there. Feast your eyes and nostrils. Then I'll tell you how it happened."

My eyes gaze on the sea of white, reminiscent of an experience four years ago in Washington State. Daddy Holzclaw took me into his cherry orchard, about this same time of the year, and sang phrases from A. E. Housman's *A Shropshire Lad:*

> Loveliest of trees the cherry now
> Is hung with bloom along the bough,
> And stands above the woodland ride
> Wearing white for Eastertide.

He loved teaching me old songs. As did Uncle Sam, Daddy Holzclaw came up with reference points about things I always try to remember. "Evocative" was always one of his key words; it meant he was going to segue— allude to other associations, challenging my mind.

I've read flowering tree descriptions by H. D. (Hilda Doolittle)—she's one of my favorite poets:

> Silver dust
> lifted from the earth,
> higher than my arms can reach,
> you have mounted.
> O silver,
> higher than my arms can reach
> you front us with great mass;
> no flower ever opened
> so staunch a white leaf,
> no flower ever parted silver
> from such rare silver,
> O white pear,
> your flower-tufts,
> thick on the branch,
> bring summer and ripe fruits
> in their purple hearts.

I tell Kahu I know about some fruit-flower poetry. He replies, "Not only poets, but also bees, butterflies, and birds enjoy fragrant flowers. Effervescent white *palama* blossoms are a feast to the eyes. They preclude the joy fruit brings to palates."

Kahu and I are talking in the kind of language Daddy Holzclaw might've used. Just because he is a little menehune doesn't mean Kahu is short on poetic language and long words. He expands my vocabulary as if he's a supplementary Uncle Sam.

Kahu explains: "Under the supervision of your great-uncle Albert Kuali'i Lyman, head of the U.S. Army Corps of Engineers, the Civilian Conservation Corps planted over sixteen thousand plum trees now blooming. Fruit was intended for residents."

I knew about the "CCC," another of President Roosevelt's ideas that pleased Ma Holzclaw. Young, unemployed men worked on conservation projects in rural areas for about a dollar a day. "A lot of money when there was no money," she'd said.

From her I learned that the CCC operated numerous conservation projects, including prevention of soil erosion and the impounding of lakes. They planted trees like these, built roads, and even did beekeeping to help pollinate plants for fertilization and reproduction. "Bees make lots of fruit possible," she explained. "Daddy depends on them, and that's why we have hives." And that's why curious me had bee stings.

I'd visited the CCC camp on the Big Island in the Volcano area. Mother stopped to see some of her clients' sons who wore uniforms and lived under quasimilitary discipline. Many joined the army at eighteen, even before this war.

"Sit here, the children are coming," Kahu says obliquely.

Miki perks up. Two persons walking up the rise definitely are not "the children."

One is a Munchkin! Others might call him a dwarf, but having seen *The Wizard of Oz* movie and reading so many Baum books, I know exactly what he is. This slim, middle-aged man with white flowing hair and a beard wears a dark blue wizard's hat. The hat extends his height, adding a rakish look to his outfit of blue jeans, *palaka* shirt, and ankle-high work boots. He has on plantation-style dress-up clothes; the cotton shirt is the traditional plaidlike woven pattern of blue-and-white checkered stripes, running vertically or horizontally, depending how your gaze falls on it.

He walks hand-in-hand with an exquisite Japanese girl resembling a youthful sprite drawn in Arthur Rackham's magical way. That nineteenth-century English fairytale artist illustrated many of my favorite books: Wagner's *The Ring of Nibelung, Peter Pan, Gulliver's Travels,* and *Rip Van Winkle,* among others.

Seeing her perks up the hungover leprechaun. Miki declaims ardently:

> Her elegant, slender little figure,
> Full of dainty grace flutters into view,
> She's so soft and warm and full of secrets.
> Her warm-hued skin, rose and nut-brown tinted,
> Oval formed face, features regular,
> Countenance expressive, interesting,
> Black eyebrows overarch sparkling dark eyes,
> Childishly pouting lips. Yoe! Yoe!
> Fresh and delicate, voluptuous grace.

"Should I be hearing this?" I ask Kahu.

"I think not," he replies and admonishes: "Hush, Miki! This time you're not even in rhyme."

Kahu explains the arrivals. They seat themselves a short distance from us. "That beardedman's Per'fessor. Raised by American Indians and he fought on their side against the U.S. Cavalry. After the Sioux Indian Wars, he joined Buffalo Bill's Wild West Show. Then he used one of Dartmouth College's Indian scholarships and continued going to school until he knew so much history that he was dubbed 'The Professor.' We refer to him as 'Per'fesser.' He came to visit Hawai'i and, as often happens to haole, he never left.

Kahu speaks quickly instead of in his usual laconic style. I guess he must want me to grasp the background before whatever we're here to see begins. I sense the Munchkin will be included in our adventure.

That young woman who perked Miki up wears a two-piece sarong, probably of silk; it clings to her body as do Queen Esther's gowns. It has a green and caramel floral pattern, and the skirt length reaches the floor; her open top has a matching bra. I gained all this fashion awareness from listening to Aunt Eva, head womens' wear buyer for Bullocks Department Store.

"Striking, isn't she?" Kahu says. "Queen Esther gave her 'clothes sense.' She's in a different color outfit every time I see her. Her name, 'Aiko,' is Japanese for 'A loved child.'

"Per'fesser took her from a family of plantation workers when she was a little child. Her parents were working near here at Koloa Sugar Plantation around 1890. By the way, that plantation used aqueducts menehune originated.

"When she was two years old, her parents went to work, leaving her in the care of her two older brothers and sisters. They went after '*ōpae* in a stream. Per'fesser, awed by her beauty, dropped a lei upstream, Aiko wandered out to catch it while her brothers' and sisters' backs were turned, and Per'fesser quickly grabbed her and took her away. Because she was holding the pretty lei, she didn't cry. Her siblings and family thought she fell in and was taken down the stream.

"Per'fesser took her to Kupuna and asked her to raise Aiko to become a youg menehune woman. When Nikko was 21, Per'fesser asked Kupuna's permission to marry Aiko. She granted it, he asked Aiko to marry him, even though he was stuck in being 35-years old with a prematurely grey beard he grew to look like a wise academician. He claims it made an impression at Dartmouth. Actually, he's really full of mischief, but his humor's not like Miki's' he's more 'polite and erudite' is the way he explains it.

"They had a marvelous wedding. Maybe at another occasion I will take you back in time to see it. Charming Menehune wedding ceremonies are unlike any other because we marry *forever and ever!*

"As man and wife, they remain inseparable and could serve as role a model for humans," he adds. Per'fesser paints endless scenes of her in beautiful clothes and without any."

I sputter, "Kahu, you are spoofing! If Per'fesser grabbed Aiko in the 1890s or so, when she was two, she would be more than eighty years old now. Aiko seems barely twenty! And you want *me* to believe what you show and tell? By the way, I *have been taken to museums* and read in classical books that a beautiful human body is the rarest art object."

Kahu smiles, then explains: "Aiko exemplifies something you will learn today about menehune. We *choose* our age. Even those entering our life, learn to exist as we do. Once you're with menehune, you select the age you want to be. Artist Perf'esser idolizes her as his young adult wife,. She'll remain that way for eternity. Once you pick what menehune age you want to be, you're stuck there and can't become younger again."

"Does this mean I'll always be ten years old?"

"No. Your destiny is in the human world. It is why I am your Kahu. You'll become mostly grown up because there are things we need you to do among Big People."

That sounds ominous. At least I'll grow up.

Per'fesser and Aiko sit closely together, chitchatting.

Giggling and chattering sounds reach us. A stately elderly menehune woman, about Aunty Kalei's age, strides out from the underbrush. Excited children, some of whom don't look a bit Hawaiian, follow her. They carry what appear to be musical instruments.

This seems a reenactment of *The Pied Piper of Hamelin*—except the original piper was the only one with a flute.

In the clearing, just above us, the elderly menehune sits down and begins to play her nose flute. The seven children form a semicircle around her.

"Can they see us?" I ask.

"No, Kupuna has cast a spell and they'll concentrate only on her. This is an important orientation. She doesn't want distractions.

"The *'ohe hano ihu* Kupuna plays has an enchanting sound, don't you think?"

I nod.

"*'Kupuna'* means 'an honored ancestor, a source for knowledge. Her garment is called a *kīhei*. See how one end covering a shoulder is tied in a knot and the other is open?"

A Hawaiian history book in mother's collection has drawings by eighteenth-century English artists. In one of them, a voluptuous young Hawaiian female exposes a breast from one side of her *kīhei*. "This common practice was considered coquettishness," explained the caption.

Mother's books in the spare room are opening my mind in ways she may not know. Dr. Mendelson is probably aware of my curiosity.

"Kupuna wears a *maile* and *mokihana* lei, picked where it is cool and damp," Kahu says. "*Maile* is profuse, of course, around our Big Island enclave. *Mokihana*, Kaua'i's island flower, similarly represents wild rain forests. Its greenish-yellow, anise-scented seed capsules resemble pearls. We'll take them back for Queen Esther to dry and use as sachet for her gowns."

He explains, "Kupuna is about to deliver a history lesson. The children will participate. You've eaten a mango and will understand everything she says."

A menehune boy carrying an *ipu,* a gourd drum, places it in front of Kupuna.

Kahu whispers, "Kupuna varies the pace of her chant; her nose flute will create both wailing and lighthearted sounds; she'll strike the *ipu* with her hands to emphasize parts of her story."

Another older boy hands her some stones; with one in each hand, she goes "click, click." I assume Kupuna is a one-woman band.

But no: The children hold musical instruments.

One of the boys had come on the scene lugging part of a tree trunk that I realize is a hollow drum.

"The drumhead is covered with taut shark skin," Kahu explains. She'll direct the drummer by nods of her head;

one to start, one to halt, another to resume drumming, and so forth. Every head movement is an instruction."

A girl with a bamboo nose flute sits facing her. The flute appears to be about one and a half spans long, about an inch in diameter.

Kahu whispers an explanation: "Along the flute tube is the hole into which the girl will breathe through her nose to blow out the music. One end of the tube is closed. At about the middle of the flute are other holes she'll finger to make the different notes."

"That boy on the left holds another type of flute he'll place between his lips and trill. Next to him also is a trumpet made by ripping a ti leaf along the middle ridge, then rolling the leaf. He will vary the sounds by moving his fingers up and down the leaf."

Three girls with ukuleles sit directly in front of Kupuna. I ask, "Isn't the string section modern?"

"Yes. Kupuna allows the girls to strum during interludes because they're such good players.

"Listen carefully," Kahu advises. "Kupuna will teach history. She's trained the children to perform orchestral background music to augment her chanting.

Children are too young to know how to perform the elaborate and ancient method she uses. Chanting was the ancient way. No one in Hawai'i sang until missionaries introduced it.

"She'll click stones to set each part of the drama's pace, use her nose flute to simulate either wailing or lighthearted skipping sounds, and she'll beat the *ipu* to announce transitions.

Now I catch on: I'm going to experience a *Menehune Opera*! This will be a drama with enchanted words and music intertwined.

As the orchestra tunes up, Kahu explains: "This will be *mo'olelo*—historical folklore that is told only during the day. Until she authorizes a break, everyone must stay in place, no one may move in front of her.

"Like a *kapu?*"

"Yes," Kahu answers.

She begins: Click, click the stones, a nod, drummers start beating, she moves her chin up and down to establish the tempo. She raises her hands, click-clicking two stones in each, like castanets. The orchestra plays the overture; she conducts by nodding her head and raising her hands to click the tempo of the next movement—then she lowers them.

Instruments underscore dramatic moods: flutes, calmness; ti-leaf trumpet, screams; flute, pastoral feelings or wailing; drums, excitement and emotion.

With her nose flute, Kupuna establishes a singing melody, while other flutists reinforce it—as if she were the lead violinist in a string orchestra.

She directs the orchestra through the melodic and rhythmic themes that'll be in her story. I know about overtures from being a violinist in a children's symphony.

"This prelude, or overture, is a musical summary of what she will chant," Kahu whispers.

"Here's the synopsis: We came from Asia, populated the Pacific, were chased by giants, and voyaged until we found Kaua'i. It was menehune Paradise for a very long time."

Kupuna lowers her head when the orchestra finishes and is contemplative.

She raises it and chants, doing marvelous things with her voice—trilling sweet melodies, wailing, uttering hiccuplike sounds, shrieking, dropping to a low register, sounding like a man, then humming, denoting calmness.

Sitting there, she dramatizes every part of the story, expressing forms of emotion within a four-octave range, as Yma Sumac, the four-octave singer, does on the radio. That Peruvian is becoming famous.

Kupuna varies her chanting style, depending on what's being expressed: She keeps a single tone for historical information, so words will be easily understood; at times she holds her voice in her throat for a rich sound. She repeats things, adding phonetic patterning for parallel information. Some portions are rhythmical, some conversational. Kupuna enunciates very carefully.

Thanks to the mango and her clear enunciation, I understand both the words and the emotions she is conveying. She varies her language: short phrases and prolonged vowels, sometimes with a fluctuating trill. Her strained guttural tones denote intensity, adding to the drama.

Kupuna's styles, moods, and pace express tenderness as well as rhythmic swing.

She intermingles tempo: duplex, slow, languid, presto. I recognize the musical techniques and understand the story:

> Walk across Asian Plains
> Into Indonesia
> Two million years ago,

Life in Java's forests.
Dragons and elephants
Some of them we hunted,
Some of them hunted us.
Using stone tools, we built
Sturdy dugout canoes,
Fish and cultivate food
—Good life for little ones
Until Big People come.
We hid in the forests,
Put canoes into caves.
They stole our food and
Wanted *to dine on us!*

Looking at the boy with a ti-leaf trumpet next to him, she drops her chin. He picks it up, blows a blood-curdling shriek, other flute players join in! Kupuna nods; they put their instruments down, she continues:

Pele passed on the word:
We now must get away,
Bring canoes from hiding,
Fill them all with our food,
Carry to the lagoon,
And soon on a dark night,
To safety we will go.
Some stuck to old habits,
Stay, acting as Hobbits.
Most paddled night and day,
Reaching the Marquesas
Landing on Kahiki,
We thought we found safety.
Right for perfect living:
Lush mountains, waterfalls,
Lagoons teeming with fish.
We farmed and were happy,

Life here was very good.
Then The Big People came,
As in Java—the same:
Stealing our crops, the food,
Chasing us to devour.
But we had sail canoes,
Large, very seaworthy.
We filled canoes with yams,
Taro and plants we liked,
Other roots, drinking nuts.
Helmswoman was Pele,
Yes, the redhead herself,
Menehune ruler.
It was a revenge time:
Jets of lava gushing,
Pele hurls forth lightning.
Vomit of flames pouring.
"Farewell to Kahiki,
To savage Big People.
To our invaders."
All twelve sisters stayed close
During the long voyage.
Hiʻiaka, the wisest,
Was in Pele's quarter.
The Pacific's Vikings
With full sails unfurled,
Into the Triangle.
Many little islands,
And barren, flat atolls,
No coconuts, water,
Only bitter *noni*.
Without volcano base,
Can't hide from Big People
Who follow us always.
Families with children

Wanted to reach the east,
Land on Rapa Nui,
Although no trees are there.
They'd traveled long enough,
Would settle into caves
And apply their stone art.
Making Rapa Nui
Spectacular to see.
Many taken as slaves:
Once White People arrived.
We continued northward,
And there we discovered
Paradise: Kaua'i!

Kupuna stops. She stands up. The first act is over. As she stretches, young menehune move around and chatter.

I rise, walk away for a few minutes. Aiko and the Per'fesser return with opened drinking coconuts, handing them to Miki, Kahu, and me, saying nothing, just showing pleasant expressions.

Kupuna returns to where she had been sitting; children resume their positions. No orchestra prelude this time, she performs a flute solo. Beethoven's *Pastoral Symphony* represented his love for nature—its woods, trees, and rocks that provide the resonance intelligent life needs. Kupuna evokes all of that, including the dimension of the sea—just by performing on a simple reed and blowing through her nose. *Magical!*

She picks up where she left off, with menehune transitioning from Kahiki to Kaua'i:

Life on the Marquesas,
Shrouded in cloud cover,

Moist, wild, rugged, and lush,
We thought it Paradise,
But neighbors made it bad.
Paradise was regained
On bounteous Kaua'i!
Menehune are strong,
Taught to be industrious,
Faithful and obedient.
Lived in caves, hollow logs,
No cliff too steep to climb,
Grew taro, yams, and ferns,
In hollows on the cliffs,
In *pali* and in swamps.
We planted breadfruit trees,
Banana rarities.
At springs, we built stones up
For sharing good water.
We built ditches to bring
Water to taro fields.
Created protein ponds—
Raise shellfish and fresh fish.
We constructed *heiau*
To honor the spirits
Who'd made Kaua'i's wonders
That we sought to enhance.
Cutting part of a point
We built a safe harbor
And canoe landing point.
We had a simple law:
Braggarts, evildoers
Become turned into stone.
Ha! Ku'aho'a,
The Hanalei Giant,
Became a stone mountain!
Pele chose Hawai'i

To make that island grow.
(Big People don't link her
To us menehune—
 She, being *powerful*.)
Her son, Menehune,
And her daughter Laka:
Pele's gentle contrasts.
The reason is because
Her children are like us.
Once the Big People came
Nothing remained the same:
They were stealing our food
And forcing us to build
Ditches, walls, and *heiau*.
We couldn't fight with them.
Not that we feared them—
Hated being near them.
Becoming "of the night,"
Disappearing from sight,
And soon they forgot us.
We're too many to stay,
Crops and fishponds are robbed.
Where we fish, all plundered.
Bananas in the hills,
And shrimp in hidden ponds,
Became sole sustenance.
"Can't stand this existence,"
Shouted out our king.
You with Hawaiian wives
Are changing what we are.
"Now, my proclamation:
'The male population
Appear on full-moon night.'
This is your king's command!"
We come and hear his plan:

"To keep our race distinct
We must find other lands.
Leave the *kanaka* wives,
Take only older sons.
Food planted and now ripe
Stays for your wives and kids.
We'll leave tomorrow night.
Take food for a few days."
Our king separates men:
In twenty divisions
With sixteen thousand each,
some half-grown boys and girls.
King's own companions are:
Kahuna, soothsayers,
Astrologer, singers,
Fun-makers, musicians,
And storytellers, too.
Then, the many thousands—
Menehune away.

Kupuna nods her head at the large boy holding the conch shell. He blows three sustained notes. The second act is over.

Children in the orchestra sit quietly, as do I.

After a brief break, Kupuna raises her head, click-clicks the stones in her hand signaling transition into the third act, and begins chanting:

Where did so many go?
Some went to nearby Necker,
Refuge place for a while,
Left their religious shrines,
Continued on their way.
New Zealand was said to be
The big new Promised Land,

Larger, and like Kaua'i,
Volcanic, grand.
Some found other places
Within small colonies,
Transient little people
Throughout the big, wide sea.
I will explain some more.
Now, you begun to know
Of origins and lore.

She rises, walks down the hill, then into the bushes; the children follow.
The *Menehune Opera* is over.
Kahu and Miki talk with Per'fesser.
I daydream.

15. Where Time's Timeless

I am unaware of time lapses. I don't know if the *Menehune Opera* was as long as Richard Wagner's Ring Cycle—*Der Ring des Nibelungen*—or if it happened in the blink of an eye. Time is inconsequential with menehune. Auntie Kalei said menehune accomplished their magnificent building projects in one night. *That was in human time.* How long did it take in menehune time?

Menehune time? Things may happen with the blink of a human eye, but menehune s-t-r-e-t-c-h every second.

It's exactly opposite to Rip Van Winkle's experiences in the Catskill Mountains. After watching ghosts of Henry Hudson's crew play ninepins, he took a nap. When he woke and returned to his hometown, *twenty years* had passed!

W. B. Yeats, poet and fairy folklore expert, explains that if a human watches elves dance on a rath, he might discover the few hours spent with them would be many years in the real world.

My experience is the contrary! What happens among them—seemingly ephemeral—extends beyond human time. They compress and accomplish so much in such little time.

Time I spend with menehune, seemingly, is *no time* in the real world.

The *Menehune Opera*'s emotional effect will surely merge into a mosaic to help me understand what being menehune means.

I ask Kahu, "The menehune king was adamant about preserving a distinct menehune race. Some of the children performing the *Menehune Opera* didn't look as if they came from the Hawaiian mothers who stayed when menehune left."

"I'll have to jump centuries ahead to explain them. When Tahitians arrived to become Hawaiians, they were isolated from the rest of the world until Captain Cook discovered Hawai'i in 1778. Spaniards passed by earlier, as Kuali'i experienced. A Spanish brother and sister survived a shipwreck off the Kona Coast and their blond hair remains. Your friend Billy is a descendent—a Hawaiian boy with curly blond locks whose family has lived 'forever' by the Kona shore.

"But it was Captain Cook, not Spaniards, who put Hawai'i on the world map; within sailors' and whalers' bodies came the Western World's deadly diseases that devastated islanders who had not built up immunities.

"Measles virus carried in the air made menehune sterile."

"You have no children, Kahu?"

"Just you."

"What about those in the orchestra?"

I've read about children choosing to enter enchanted lands: Puppet-boy Pinocchio hangs out with Foolish Boys and almost becomes a donkey. Lost Boys join Peter Pan. In *A Midsummer Night's Dream,* Fairy King Oberon and Queen Titania argue over a human baby they acquire.

Kahu reads my mind: "Menehune do not steal children. Per'fesser was a haole from the mainland when he grabbed Aiko; he followed what fairies elsewhere practice. He didn't realize that wasn't our custom.

"We wanted to expand our thin numbers. Miki said European fairies replace infants with a changeling."

"I've heard of them, but please explain."

"Fairies spot a suitable baby and spirit it away. An old fairy takes its place. The fairy becomes a changeling—it changes to resemble the baby. A century or more older than the baby it replaces, the changeling is inclined to be cranky and impatient. Not every adult wants to be constantly treated like a child. The parents wonder, 'What happened to our sweet little innocent? Why is it bored and ill-tempered?' Miki cautioned, 'While fairies enjoy a new, sweet little innocent addition, the changeling usually is found out and fairies have to replace the baby. It is not a satisfactory arrangement.'

"Picking up orphan Hawaiian babies wasn't an option. Someone was usually eager to *hānai*—to foster a child needing a home—sort of like you were from time to time. We rejected the changeling concept. Miki helped in another way."

"How was that?"

"When Catholic priests came to Hawai'i, Miki peeked in on their proselytizing. He heard them speak of *limbus infantium*—'The Limbo of Infants.'"

This strikes a responsive chord.

Mother drove ahead of the "commodities truck" that delivered monthly groceries to persons "on relief." Some of her clients, who were unable to write their names, made an "X" mark on a Territory of Hawai'i delivery receipt and she'd attest to it. She couldn't write her name either, but added the "X" maker's name in her italic-printing style and included her initials.

I went along to a commodity delivery at the Painted Church in South Kona where Father John, a Belgian priest and self-taught artist, had painted part of the inside of the wooden-frame church to resemble Heaven. He included some of the saints.

While I was studying Heaven, I overheard Mother tell the priest, "We lived with a Catholic family when Arthur was an infant. Fearing he might die from a severe asthma attack, the family asked a priest to baptize him."

Right there, where I could overhear him, the priest told Mother: "The baptism was to assure Arthur would go to Heaven."

Kahu breaks in on my daydream.

"After listening to priests, Miki said we should send a recruiting team to Limbo."

"Please, explain this to me."

"Miki had heard a priest say that Limbo of Infants is where the unbaptized who die in infancy go. They are too young to have committed personal sins but are not freed from original sin because *they* haven't had the baptismal ceremony.

"The Priest said Limbo is a state of maximum natural happiness—although not quite Heaven.

"Miki came up with the idea of inviting some of those Innocents to Hawai'i. Every so often a group of us go there to recruit. Since they're almost like angels, we have to tell them honestly about the downside of living as menehune: Being ignored, unseen, and blamed for things that disappear. It's pretty nice up there, so Hawai'i is a real hard sell."

I'd seen *The Blue Bird* movie, starring Shirley Temple. Very loving and sentimental, it was running about the same time as *The Wizard of Oz*. Aunt Eva bought me a book of Maurice Maeterlinck's play, on which the movie was based. In it, a good fairy helps Mytyl and her brother Tyltyl find the lost bluebird of happiness. Along the way, they visit a place similar to Heaven where children wait to be born.

Seeing the movie and reading the play made me realize not everyone wants to leave a place where they are happy to go to the unknown. A boy and girl in the movie did not want to be born—it meant they probably would never see each other.

Per'fesser and Aiko walk away as I hear about "recruiting." Believing I've done enough reflecting, Kahu suggests we join them, explaining, "From me you learn about Hawai'i; Per'fesser helps you know about the world. His cave is a painterly studio, not a queen's chamber. No need to be shy."

Trot, trot—up the mountain he goes, with me following at his heels. The sun is starting to descend and twilight is setting in. Suddenly companions appear, glowing like fireflies—pretty winged fairies speeding alongside us, darting ahead, sitting on leaves and pushing their glow signals up a few wattages, then soaring in the air and swooping down and waving their wings. Their quick movements remind me of hummingbirds.

I scurry to keep up with Kahu. The little fairies perch on leaves at the cave's opening, wiggling their wings, twinkling, and glowing like magical sentinels. Miki winks and says, flirtatiously:

> Hello dears, you'll enjoy what I wrote to hear.
> I'll set my hat near for you to guard here.

As usual, his verse gets worse when pretties excite him. We walk into an art museum exalting Aiko. Taped to the wall on my right are black and white sketches. Color paintings of her, placed on easels, are everywhere. Framed oil paintings hang on the wall's other three sides. Some are attached to the cave ceiling.

Aiko is pensive and unsmiling in several, a calm counterpoint to the dramatic landscapes and vagaries of nature surrounding her—dark clouds, fog, lightning, rain, a rainbow, brilliant rays of sunlight. She stands nude to her waist in ocean foam in one; adjacent is a freshwater counterpart of her bathing in a pond, waterfall in the background. I remembered visiting museums and being told, "The human form is the most exquisite and challenging art subject."

Per'fesser created close-ups in which she stares directly at the viewer. A black-and-white sketch shows only her shadow on a tree. One of the largest paintings is a standing profile of Aiko staring into Waimea Valley, skirt billowing in the breeze.

She is shown nude in a series of studies—face down sleeping on a *lauhala* mat, shaded by a tree; sitting by a mountain pool among strewn flowers. One dramatizes shadow patterns on her body.

Per'fesser ran out of space and taped some paintings to the top of the cave; others are rolled up and stacked against its sides.

Aiko's a chirpy hostess. She says, "Per'fesser has prepared carefully for this show-and-tell. Sit here, Miki. Kahu, this spot is for you. Arthur, use this stool in front of the screen."

The screen is a white sheet hanging from the top of the cave to the ground. Aiko smiling once we're in place, walks to a magic lantern projector. Looking carefully, I realize it is an elaborate version of kerosene hurricane lanterns the Holzclaws had used. The base of the projector is filled with kerosene. Aiko lights a wick, and its mirrors and magnifying lenses enlarge and project onto the sheet images Per'fesser has painted onto the slides.

Per'fesser, standing to my left so as not to block the screen, explains: "Kahu asked me to provide world perspectives to improve your understanding and appreciation."

I like that direct, focused way of speaking; it's not stuffy, theoretical, or condescending. That's how kids like to hear things.

"You are writing a journal, Arthur?"

I nod.

"Eventually, will you allow others to read it?"

I nod again.

"Good—others can trail labyrinths you've explored and perhaps find further truths. Let me serve as a sorcerer."

"Like Merlin?"

"In some respects. I will be a source for information and other viewpoints, as Merlin did with Arthur, who even explored the animal kingdom." He points his finger in the air. "But I promise not to turn you into a 'Wart.' I want you to gain *perspective.* Do you know that word?"

"Yes, I do."

"Well then, *perspective* helps to understand things, sometimes in new ways. Think of it as a *root word* having embedded meanings. This root word contains *pers,* an abbreviation for person and personal. It has *spec,* which means both speculate and see. It includes *tive,* which sounds like "is, live, and id." (He uses an *eh* sound for the *i.*) "Use that to think of *live*"—like in *alive.*" (This time he uses a long *i.*)

I nod my head.

"You should explore and extend your *perspective.* Do you understand my wordplay?"

"I think so. Perspective will contribute to what I see and understand and how I respond."

"Yes. Now I will augment the *Menehune Opera.*"

Aiko inserts a glass slide into the magic lantern, fiddles with the wick, and a full-color illustration fills the makeshift screen.

Per'fesser begins: "Kupuna left these predecessors out of the *mo'olelo*. The large figure represents Nāwao, Kaua'i's first arrival. Nāwao were large, wild creatures who lived in upland forests and came out only at night. In that respect, they were like European trolls who turned to stone when caught by the light of day. There are storytellers who claim large hills on this island once were living, breathing Nāwao. Bands of quick-witted, aggressive menehune probably exterminated them by confusing and chasing them over cliffs.

"The two smaller creatures on the screen represent Nāwao descendents. To the left is a Mū, the silent bug-eyed ones. To the right is a Wa, the shouters. They were vegetarians who browsed for bananas and grubbed for the taro and sweet potato roots menehune grew."

Aiko inserts a new glass slide that shows menehune in loincloths pointing farming staves and stone tools at several naked, hairy Wa and Mū.

"Accidental meetings, as this illustrates, were probably as startling to one group as to the other. Fishing and farming made menehune sharper witted and they had tools for weapons. You see silent Mū grabbing whatever rocks they can to scare away menehune approaching them with upraised hoes. The Wa are blustering and threatening as their females scurry off with babies, giving them a headstart in running away from menehune, which is what both male Mū and Wa are about to do.

"Menehune cut bunches of green fruit from banana trees and hung them to ripen in their caves so Mū and Wa wouldn't have food. Menehune found ways to frighten them away from land they wanted to cultivate. Constant pressure from growing numbers of menehune and decreasing freedom of movement caused Mū and Wa to disappear."

Aiko inserts another glass slide of two adjoining landmasses; the bottom one resembles North America.

Per'fesser explains: "Arthur, whether it was Eden or Africa out of which they came, the human race traveled far. This shows the Bering Straits that linked the Asian and North American continents between 5 to 1.8 million years ago. The straits enabled human migration from Asia.

"There were other land bridges. For instance, the British Isles, with a dry bed on the site of the English Channel, was an extension of continental Europe."

Aiko replaces the slide with another of Per'fesser's illustrations.

"Here you see the dry basin of the China Sea linking Sumatra, Java, and Borneo to the Asian mainland. Australia joined with Antarctica and also led to New Guinea and Tasmania."

Per'fesser nods, and Aiko turns off the projector. He continues: "Kupuna described menehune life in Java, then migration to the Marquesas, and ultimately here, to Hawai'i. Pacific wanderers also went to Sumatra, Java, Borneo, and the Philippines; eastward to New Guinea, the Carolines, the Solomons, the New Hebrides, Fiji, Samoa, Tahiti, the Marquesas; and north to the Gilbert and Marshall Island groups. Little people settled in some of these areas.

"Menehune ancestors were intelligent and used tools to compensate for their modest physique. This is *not* hearsay: Archeologists discovered a 'Java Man' in 1891. More findings in the early 1930s suggested Java's fertility for anthropological research, but the war halted it.

"Once scientists unearth tools, they will recognize that little people hunted 2,200-pound elephants, Komodo dragons, and they will realize menehune ancestors crossed two water barriers over 840,000 years ago to get there from mainland Asia. Although having brains the size of a three-year old child, these little people may amaze Big People by their accomplishments.

"Menehune were never safe. They were followed by others wanting what they discovered and developed. Some humans, especially those in the Marquesas, were voracious cannibals. And I can't begin to think of being a tender little person in Melanesia!

Miki speaks up:

> Hide when a Big Person happens to say,
> 'We'll have you over for dinner someday.'

Pretending not to have heard, Per'fesser announces, rather grandly, "Aiko will project my interpretation of what I expect Miki will describe in a gentlemanly manner." He stares intensely at Miki while stressing *gentlemanly*.

Aiko projects Per'fesser's painting of a fairy procession within an enchanted forest. The beautiful fairy queen and attendants, on horseback, are accompanied by masses of fairies, some playing musical instruments. The painting portrays so much: Rich colors, seductive women, figures of many sizes, and varieties of costumes. The keen expressions on all faces reveal that Per'fesser is a master of Pre-Raphaelite fairy art.

Miki is awed. He stares, mouth agape, looking toward Per'fesser, who has a very pleased smile; he nods.

I turn momentarily. The winged fairies are peeking in the cave entrance and flicker excitedly as they see counterparts seemingly glowing on the screen. Regaining his composure, Miki lowers his voice; he speaks conversationally. But he doesn't sound like Miki:

> Kupuna's words cast a magical spell,
> Ignoring all worlds save one she knows well,
> Her stories, enchanting each childish mind,
> Explaining what in Hawai'i they'll find.
> But Attah, you have read much *more* than most
> And from Grandpa learned of "The Holy Ghost."
> Here's the big picture—it never varies:
> *Menehune are Hawai'i's fairies!*

He pauses for dramatic effect. Kahu and Per'fesser quietly say something to each other. Miki continues in a quiet, secretive voice, conveying mystery and awe—one might say "It is awesome and then some."

His is the "Lamont Cranston" sound that opens network radio broadcasts of *The Shadow*.

Miki usually speaks in a shrill, sometimes grating tenor. Did he learn to drop his voice at the Globe Theatre, where Will Shakespeare's versatile male actors originally played both male and female roles? Words flowing from his "baritone" have an unworldly mysteriousness:

> Fairies are beings having human forms
> Whose power is greater than mankind's norms.
> Fairy-folk roamed freely among mankind
> Before the world was changed by human mind.

Once, in the dreaming dawn of history,
Between our worlds there lay no mystery.
Fluid fairy nature marked by caprice,
Using human form splendid or grotesque.
Before boundaries became a bother
'Twixt the mortal world and any other,
Fairies' complex and busy lives went on,
Our realm endowed with added dimension.
Fairy existence in a human form:
Splendid or grotesque—we followed no norm.
Also took shapes of animals or birds,
Flames, plants, or flowers, whatever urges.
Between one blink of the eye and the next
We made ourselves unseen, humans to vex.
Ambiguous we were among mortals:
Woe to unwary entering our portals.
Adventures with a mortal and fairy
Often became fraught with uncertainty.
I coaxed The Master to visit Ireland
On a Midsummer Eve, he, being my friend,
Across the meadows of Connacht we came.
Then what happened made him never the same:
Darkness deepens, the silver moon glimmers,
From a cluster of trees harp strings shimmer,
Flutes releasing sweet liquid, shining runs,
Belled bridles herald an approach that comes,
A splendid column rides from the forest,
Gold-clad knights on white horses coming forth,
With a bevy of princesses, seeing
Inclined graceful necks and eyes that gleamed:
Casting intense wild looks and causing sighs.
Made Will tremble, a glaze came to his eyes,
And his heart contracted with deep longing
While they passed from sight into the gloaming.
He was among the last of all mortals

To see fairies passing between portals:
We had begun our retreat from mankind—
Rarely, will fairies humans again find.
As the natural world was being tamed,
The fairies it once sheltered soon became
Evermore unseen elusive strangers.
(My going with Will spared any dangers.)
Will was able to express the delight,
He preserved mysterious Midsummer Night.
I am his merry wanderer of that night,
"Robin Goodfellow" an actor so bright,
Who causes confusion among mankind
Whose follies entertain me all the time.
Kupuna uses Hawaiian sayings,
Per'fesser states his history claimings,
But know yourself, this truth never varies:
Menehune are Hawai'i's fairies!

Per'fesser nods approvingly; Aiko turns off the projector. We say our thanks and quickly leave, with stirred emotions. It is twilight. Fairies at the entrance swoop around, ready to guide us away. Miki speaks quietly to Kahu, then picks up his hat from the cave entrance and wanders into the bushes.

"Miki wants to gather some *mokihana* for Queen Esther," Kahu tells me. "We'll start—he'll catch up."

Sure enough, after we've gone around a few bends, he's back, his hat filled to the brim with fragrant *mokihana* berries to scent the queen's garment collection.

"Quick pick," he confides to me in his normal high-pitched voice.

Home from Kaua'i, at the eucalyptus tree, Kahu says, "We won't travel for a while. Reflecting on the past will broaden your *perspective*. That's the word the Per'fesser used. Think about experiences before you met us. They may have created your affinity. Your brain is becoming overloaded. Describe life before being menehune.

So *that's* what I'll journalize about now: About becoming an early and avid reader and how this nurtured my imagination leading me to creative experiences that otherwise I might never see. My "perspectives" began at age three.

16. Mind Gardening

My entrance into the world of imagination began with *A Child's Garden of Verses.* Uncle Sam guided me through it after Cowboy Monkey and Piggy were gone. Three years old, I was living with my grandparents when the doctor told them, "Kapok stuffing makes his asthma worse." When I awoke one morning and my pals weren't there, I was disconsolate!

Buying the illustrated poetry book to cheer me up, Uncle Sam helped me recognize and say words within it. I memorized lines.

Author Robert Louis Stevenson described his "pleasant land of counterpane":

> When I was sick and lay a-bed
> I had two pillows at my head,
> And all my toys beside me lay,
> To keep me happy all the day.

I spent days in bed, but my toys were gone.

Uncle Sam introduced me to Eugene Field's "Little Boy Blue," and I realized Cowboy Monkey and Piggy missed me too:

> Ay, faithful to Little Boy Blue they stand,
> Awaiting the touch of a little hand,
> The smile of a little face.

Learning to read with Uncle Sam leading me through books having lots of words on a page, I instinctively adopted authors' language, rhythm, and rhyme. Hans Christian Andersen's enchanting fairy tales weren't insurmountable; neither were the Brothers Grimm's scary ones.

I became healthier and waited on the front porch for Uncle Sam to return from school. I'd follow him around until, handing me a book, seating me close to his desk, he settled me down to experience what poet John Donne described:

> I, the shadow, tread
> And to brave clearness
> All things were reduced.

"What's this word mean?" I asked, as Uncle Sam did homework. A student at Punahou, a fine private Honolulu school, he always had lots of studying to do.

He'd write the word in a notebook, then act it out. Uncle Sam quizzed me on words in the notebook so I'd remember to use them.

"It'll build your vocabulary," he explained.

He grinned broadly as I mimicked his mnemonic hooks. Our exchanges were similar to this one:

"Uncle Sam, what's 'resound?' This sentence reads: 'Rapunzel let her sweet voice *resound*.'"

"Resound is to fill a place with sound—it's similar to an echo."

Using a memory-locking trick, he shouted "*Resound!*" into cupped hands, amplifying it.

Uncle Sam explained: "An echo reflects sound waves from a surface back to the listener. I'll take you up to Kaimukī's empty reservoir tomorrow, and you can yell into it so your voice will echo (clasping his hands again) . . . and *resound!*"

At another time I asked, "What does *'creep'* mean? I thought it was an 'icky' person, but here's how this story goes: "'*Creep* in," said the witch, "and see if the oven is heated properly. Let me show you how."'"

Uncle Sam abruptly fell to the floor. On his knees, with both hands, he lifted the desk chair overhead. He pretended to shuffle under it and explained, "I am the witch *creeping* into the oven."

He shoved the chair to the floor: *"BANG!"* This dramatized Gretel's slamming the oven door behind the creepy, crafty, creeping witch—then baking her into gingerbread!

Grandma said his severe acne made Uncle Sam shy. He came home right after school, stuck around on weekends, and never begrudged my trailing him.

During our tandem explorations of the Brothers Grimm's fairy tales, I learned about deep malevolence, that heroes and heroine can become infinitely happy forever—and I realized that my dark, very Hawaiian-looking uncle *never* was at a loss for words.

Mother worked with the leper colony on Moloka'i. Kids weren't allowed there, so I lived in Honolulu with Grandpa, Grandma, Auntie Maile, and Uncle Sam. Once, when I couldn't stop crying, Maile tried shaking away my tears. Going into a choking fit, I almost passed out. Grandma was worried that Auntie Maile might accidentally hurt me.

Mother lost her job with the Territory of Hawai'i's Department of Health due to the Great Depression. "Women workers and non-locally-born males were fired first," is how she explained it to Grandma and Grandpa. Mother stayed with us for a while before finding a new job through the University of Washington's Social Work School; the university was her alma mater. I went along "because of Maile's excitable behavior." We stayed in the Seattle Salvation Army Girls Home.

I didn't understand why my first-grade teacher looked strangely after I said where I lived and explained, "My mother makes people feel better."

She told me to raise my arm and hold one finger up if I had to go to the bathroom; she'd nod her head so I wouldn't have to wet my pants—again.

I liked being the center of attention among friendly young women at the Girls Home. Singing was fun, and so were the Salvation Army officer's "Pep Talks." He'd conclude by delivering a long prayer, then he'd tell us to silently say a prayer of our own. After a minute or two, he'd raise his hand for all of us to loudly call out, "Amen." This was supposed to build enthusiasm.

Sometimes I was asked to shout out the brief little dinner grace Grandma taught me: "God is great, God is good, and we thank him for this food." *Never did I do,* "Father, Son, and Holy Ghost, she who eats the fastest eats the most!" That's what a mischievous girl urged me to recite.

Some people thought that place was for fallen women, problem girls, and outcasts.

I was having a wonderful time, liked the joyful evangelism, and would've enjoyed staying with my new "aunties," but Mother's social work job involved traveling. I was turned over to the state's foster care system.

My head was filled with notions from reading. At dusk, in the pullout bed at my foster home, I stared at fairy and pixie patterns on the bedroom's rosy-hued wallpaper, hoping Wynken, Blynken, and Nod might take me into Eugene Field's enchanted places:

> Wynken and Blynken are two little eyes,
> And Nod is a little head,
> And the wooden shoe that sailed the skies
> Is a wee one's trundle bed.

I knew about Robert Louis Stevenson's spooky dreamland journeys:

> But every night I go abroad
> Afar into the land of Nod. . . .
> All alone beside the streams
> And up the mountain-sides of dreams.
> The strangest things are there for me,
> Both things to eat and things to see,
> And many frightening sights abroad
> Till morning in the land of Nod.

For protection, before climbing into bed, I did as Grandma taught: "Kneel next to bed and pray for guardian-angel protection":

> Watch over me throughout the night,
> Keep me safe within your sight.

17. Entering Oz

My foster parents raised fruit, vegetables, and poultry. On the wood stove's top, without a frying pan, Ma Holzclaw fixed the biggest-ever breakfast flapjacks that had nice, crispy edges.

A block of ice in the icebox kept food fresh; the friendly iceman chipped a piece for me on delivery day. Ma Holzclaw poured syrup in a little saucer, and I'd sit on a kitchen stool to dip and lick my ice treat. Having asthma meant not having ice cream or milk, so Ma Holzclaw invented "sweet ice" for me.

Dim kerosene lamps made my head ache, limiting reading during Washington's long, dark, rainy, and snowy days. After the rural cooperative brought electricity to the house, Ma Holzclaw exulted, "Thank you President Roosevelt for advancing us from primitive American life." She said that a lot; she really appreciated him.

She bought a tall electric lamp, placed it next to a big, cozy chair, and loaned me children's books from her "teaching days."

My job was to feed the chickens—regular-sized and small Guineas. Ma Holzclaw said, "English took Guinea fowl to countries they settled. That's how they came to America, where they are a delicacy."

She liked to explain things: "Having fancy poultry is a good idea even though times are bad and they require special care. They're like the difference between 'prime' and 'choice' beef: Fresh chicken sells for twenty cents a pound; we get at least ten cents a pound more for our Guinea hens and capons. They're our goldmine."

Hmm . . . I thought. Reading "Jack and the Beanstalk" gave me the idea to shout "Fee! Fi! Fo! Fum! I smell the blood of an Englishman!" into the valuable Guinea fowl pen. Then I'd peek into nests, hoping I'd frightened those delicate, crabby hens into laying golden eggs.

After a few days of this, Ma Holzclaw called me into the house. Instead of scolding me for terrorizing her cherished flock, she pointed to a pile of books stacked next to the reading chair and wonderful electric lamp. All were by Frank Baum: *The Wizard of Oz, Dorothy and the Wizard in Oz, The Emerald City of Oz, Glenda of Oz, The Lost Princess of Oz, The Marvelous Land of Oz, Princess Ozma of Oz, The Scarecrow of Oz,* and *The Patchwork Girl of Oz.*

These stopped me from being an ogre. I went to the hen coop only to toss in some feed, having entered the Land of Oz.

Foster-child Arthur, ward of Washington State.

Until now I'd thought only Europeans wrote fairy tales. How was Mr. Baum able to interact with enchanted beings? Where are they? Were some in Washington State? Maybe I could learn to talk with totem poles when I visited Uncle Robert Armstrong in Vancouver, Canada?

Really wanting to know, I pestered Ma Holzclaw to find out about Mr. Baum in the library.

She reported that he'd also been a sickly child who was inclined to daydreaming—something I was becoming good at doing. Mr. Baum loved to stage dramas and act and was a stamp collector and dealer. While a teenager living in Chittenango, New York, he published the *Stamp Collector* magazine on his own little printing press. He also published a magazine about fancy poultry—"like our Guinea hens," she said with bit of an edge.

Ma Holzclaw later brought another Baum book from the library: *The Life and Adventures of Santa Claus.*

On my 1936 Christmas card, I wrote Grandpa exciting news: "I am now a stamp collector! Since Mr. Baum's first name is Lyman, I wonder if we're related?"

Grandpa replied, "I don't think so, because Lyman is a Christian name as well as a surname. However, Lyman Beecher and his daughter Harriett Beecher Stowe are said to be in the family."

Explaining the difference between "Christian" and "surnames," Ma Holzclaw added Stowe's book, *Uncle Tom's Cabin*, to my reading pile. I began referring grandly to its author as "Distant-Aunt Harriet."

The Holzclaws were very kind to me, but theirs was not my permanent home; I was a foster child, meaning I was in transition. I compensated with imaginary affinities, created friends in my head, replayed what I read, imitated authors' language, and built a vocabulary. In the schoolyard I learned that other kids talk with imaginary friends. "My parents say they're part of a phase I'm in," confided a chirpy little redheaded girl.

Robert Louis Stevenson had imaginary friends. He created his own world and even wrote a poem about them—"The Unseen Playmate." These lines, I was certain, pertained to me:

> When children are happy and lonely and good,
> The Friend of the Children comes out of the wood,
> He loves to be little, he hates to be big.

Gradually, book-by-book, I entered the creative zone. Why would I ever want to leave? Such a comforting, safe, secret shield should be more than just "part of a phase." Why not just love *being little?*

Grandpa wrote often. He responded to my news about Mr. Baum being a stamp collector by enclosing stamps and promising to send me a Hawai'i Clipper First-Day Issue from the Honolulu post office. It would celebrate Pan American Airways' new transpacific flying boat that landed on the ocean and served the Hawaiian Islands.

He described seeing the huge plane churning water over West Loch in Pearl Harbor, then climbing high in the sky, traveling at 175 miles an hour. "It can reach California in 18 hours. . . . That same trip took five days for you and your mother on the *Matsonia!*"

He also sent stamp-sized labels with morale-building slogans attributed to Doc R. Happy smiles on cartoon figures reinforced each label's slogan: "Good Times Are Coming Back!" Grandpa said profit from sales of these decorative labels went to the Salvation Army for its work among the unemployed.

Ma Holzlaw explained, "Doc R is Franklin D. Roosevelt and he will cure America. Oh, by the way, FDR also collects stamps."

Using his beautiful Palmer method of penmanship, Grandpa corresponded as if I were a grown-up. I tried imitating his cursive writing.

He enclosed stories he wrote about Hawaiian plants: "How the Breadfruit Tree Got Its Name," "Why the Guava Became a Strawberry," "Floating Coconuts Save a Prince."

I mentioned the Tin Man and Scarecrow in one of my letters. Grandpa probably thought those were nicknames. This was in 1936, three years before *The Wizard of Oz* movie. I provided no details of our friendship. I didn't want him to suspect they were supernatural beings, as he was adverse to all but the Holy Spirit and guardian angels.

We had rural electric but not rural telephone. Mother and I communicated by mail. Realizing I missed talking with Piggy and Cowboy Monkey, she seemed amenable to my Oz friends—probably thinking they were Holzclaw neighbors.

In one letter she described going to school in Vancouver and living with Grandma's brother Robert and his wife Mary—the Armstrongs. "It was far better than our one-room school in Kohala on the Big Island."

Mother was born left-handed, but Canadian Catholic nuns forced her to write right-handed—"The way other students did," she explained. "Sisters slapped my hand with a ruler if I didn't follow their rule. They taught 'conformity.' I couldn't do 'script' with my right hand and was able only to print each letter of the alphabet separately rather than joining them together."

Mother finished the letter with these words in her simple, slightly italicized printing style and added an underlining: "Now you are becoming good at reading <u>and writing</u>."

I learned about "layers of meanings" in Jonathan Swift's *Gulliver's Travels* while reading it under the Holzclaw's nice lamp. On the surface were adventures among diminutive people and giants, talking horses, and Japanese pirates. But it held deeper lessons about human personalities and characteristics—valuable knowledge for a charity case who was affected by others' moods.

Daddy Holzclaw said I'd enjoy exploring "knighthood." He described Siegfried, a Norseman raised by a dwarf. He explained that opera composer Richard Wagner glorified

Siegfried's exploits. Daddy loved opera. He said Siegfried found treasure, won Brunhilde, and awakened the singing Walkyrie. Siegfried's sole inheritance was a broken old sword he forged together. It made him nearly invincible. Daddy explained: "To overcome him, Hagen hid the sword and sneakily thrust a javelin in Siegfried's back."

Wagner and the Grimm Brothers knew the hidden world; I was beginning to realize it was my world, too. If ever having a magic sword, I'd be careful no one hid it from me.

"Wagner's music will stir your soul," Daddy said. "Being very young, continue enjoying Oz for now. Consider it *Ozmosis*."

Daddy Holzclaw improvised and emphasized fancy words to expand my vocabulary.

Mother's job ended abruptly in Washington: The state couldn't pay its workers and foster parents. She found another job with the State of California. I would ride a train, become that state's ward, and leave bankrupt Washington behind.

Ma and Daddy Holzclaw helped me to board the train. They told the Union Pacific train porter to look after me and slipped him some of their Guinea fowl money—I saw 'em do it. Both of their faces were very red, but they acted cheery and reminded me to "be a good boy."

Years later, I learned they'd wanted to adopt me and why they couldn't.

The porter helped me order meals in the dining car. He said to leave my ugly high-top boots below the curtained bunk bed he made up for me. "They'll be waiting here with a fresh shine in the morning."

Distant-Aunt Harriett Stowe described how Uncle Tom, a man looking like the porter, saved Little Eva. It made me feel confident I'd be safe during the train ride. He took me to the dining car and helped me order meals. I addressed him as "Mr. Porter"—what a big smile he gave!

Mr. Porter turned me over to Aunt Eva at the Los Angeles train station. Mother's tall, brunette sister had stylish bobbed black hair, dressed smart, and smelled sweet from her fancy department store's perfume. I saw her give Mr. Porter some money when shaking his hand. Aunt Eva was a buyer for the Bullock's in Los Angeles. Her husband Bob Reed was a crime reporter for the *Los Angeles Times* newspaper.

18. La-La L.A.

The Gulbranson family was my new Los Angeles foster home. Uncle Bob Reed sometimes drove me to his and Aunt Eva's apartment for an outing. Returning from one of them, he pulled into a Shell service station to gas up. Spotting me in the front seat while cleaning our windshield, the attendant said, "Hold on a minute." He hurried into the office and brought back a Treasure Island map and stickers of Mickey Mouse and his friends experiencing adventures at the upcoming 1939 World's Fair on Treasure Island.

Pointing, he said enthusiastically, "There'll be lots more stickers to put in all these blank spaces on the map's border. Keep coming back, I'll have 'em for you."

Uncle Bob kept returning so and I'd have the complete collection. He paid ten cents a gallon for gas, instead of maybe less elsewhere because California had "gas wars." Back then, Mickey Mouse was ten years old and domestic crude oil cost thirty-eight cents a barrel. That's the price Uncle Bob mentioned as we drove past drilling rigs. I remember him saying, "Isn't this wonderful? All that money comes from right out of the ocean. America needs to be rich and oil will make it happen."

When he took me to the *Los Angeles Time*'s headquarters, he said, "This is one of the most beautiful buildings in America!" Uncle Bob Reed always had a "gee whiz" enthusiastic talking manner—his newsman personality.

The lobby had floor-to-ceiling murals painted by movie art director Hugo Ballin. I studied them, reading their descriptions while Uncle Bob checked for news desk messages.

Ballin's imagery was described as "classical," radically different from the modern art done by painters decorating the walls of city post offices and other public buildings. The Works Progress Administration (WPA) hired artists to interpret American values during the depression. FDR enthusiast Ma Holzclaw explained all that to me. She said, "FDR helps artists and writers to survive."

She made me very cognizant of illustrators as well as book writers. "Authors write to open your mind, artists draw to expand and maybe color it," she explained. "Learn artists' names—they deserve fame."

Ballin's storytelling imagery appealed to me. As I studied descriptive charts explaining his scenes, my new Caucasian uncle stepped up closely to confide, "People think Eva's 'European.' We don't tell them differently. She's nicknamed 'Gypsy' because of her swarthy skin."

Why did some adults feel compelled to tell me things I did not want to know?"

Left, Arthur's mother, Ruth Hualani, had her mother's fair complexion, sister Aunt Eva, on the right, had their father's coloring.

Uncle Sam and the Holzclaws spoke at my level and explained unfamiliar words. Other grown-ups, such as my new Uncle Bob, didn't.

Aunt Eva was somewhat darker than my mother; she resembled Uncle Sam. I didn't add "swarthy" to my vocabulary list; it didn't sound flattering.

Uncle Bob allowed me to use his portable typewriter to peck out a letter to my mother.

A scrapbook sitting next to the typewriter invited me to peek inside at mounted photographs of car wrecks on Los Angeles highways. Stuck in the back were unmounted, gruesome scenes: a decapitated head in the middle of a road, a shot woman splattered in an apartment, and others like those.

Aunt Eva walked into Uncle Bob's study to see how my typing was going. She found me holding the opened scrapbook, looking puzzled.

She immediately told me to do my favorite thing: "Pour in bubble bath liquid, fill the tub to the top, get in, and relax. I'll bring you the program from *The Mikado*. Words to Ko-ko's song you like so well are in it. Soak and sing . . . 'Willow, tit-willow.' I'll run the bathwater." She spoke rapidly, as if she were upset.

The Holzclaws used an outside hand pump to fill a bucket with water, heating the bucket on the kitchen stove for "Saturday night baths." I dipped a washcloth into the bucket for a "sponge bath." In rural Washington there was no running water, no hot water heater, and only an outdoor well to collect buckets of water. President Roosevelt hadn't advanced the Holzclaws *all the way* from primitive rural life.

In Los Angeles, Aunt Eva offered me unimaginable luxury: a tub filled with hot water and bubbles up to the chin. This caused scrapbook photos to drift from my mind.

I overheard Uncle Bob apologizing to agitated Aunt Eva: "I know he's sensitive. I just forgot those were in it."

He and Aunt Eva had split by the time his book of sensational highway crash photos was published. I remembered some of the images during nightmares. The head on the road made a memorable impression.

At the Gulbransons, I concentrated on violin lessons, played in a youth orchestra, sang in an Episcopal church's boy's choir, and kept away from Jimmy, the other foster child. Three years older, he was sort of mean. Because

I was one of the choir's soloists, the church gave me a quarter each month. Ma Holzclaw's singing lessons were paying off! World War I British lead soldiers cost five cents each at the downtown Los Angeles' F. W. Woolworth five-and-dime store not far from the church. I traveled around easily on roller skates and was accumulating a nice-sized army to hide from Jimmy. Any nickel I got my hands on went for soldiers. I hoped that someday I'd have privacy to play with them.

Jimmy didn't do well in school and discouraged me from reading or practicing the violin, but I did both when he wasn't around. Mr. Jack Haley was portraying the Tin Man in *The Wizard of Oz* movie being filmed in Los Angeles for release in 1939. He may have been Jimmy's godfather. I guessed so because Mr. Haley visited often.

"Stay out of the way," Jimmy ordered whenever Mr. Haley was expected. He'd punch me on the arm for emphasis. I peeked around corners a few times. Mr. Haley seemed an ordinary human-looking person; once a vaudeville performer, he moved gracefully, in contrast to the real Tin Man in Mr. Baum's book. W. W. Denslow drew the original Tin Man as a black-and-white assemblage of tin parts; that's how he appeared clanking through my daydreams.

Everyone knew about the upcoming movie and its 124 tiny adult and some child actors. Photographs and stories about them were printed often in the *Los Angeles Times* because they were a curiosity. Steeped in fairy tales, I realized this might be the first time ordinary human beings witnessed little people busily engaged—at least since the miller's daughter spotted Rumpelstiltskin spinning gold from straw. People appearing to be "different" are often looked at as curiosities or are ostracized. Mother explained that to me at the Salvation Army Girls Home.

Schoolmates taught me that a foster child is "different." To compensate, I spent as much time as possible among nonjudgmental friends found between book covers—especially Mr. Baum's Munchkins. The newspaper said Hollywood's live Munchkins had earnest and optimistic dispositions, experienced emotional feelings, and wanted to be helpful and accepted—sort of like seven-year-old me.

In summer 1938, four years after we'd left, Mother and I returned to Hawai'i on the *Lurline,* Matson Line's most luxurious ocean liner. I had been seasick during our transpacific trip on the bumpy *Matsonia* but experienced smooth sailing on the *Lurline*. We had movies and popcorn every evening and free ice cream during the afternoon—none for me, though.

Mother had a job on the island of Hawai'i, and I could live with Grandpa and Grandma on O'ahu because Aunt Maile had moved to Kāne'ohe Mental Hospital.

Uncle Sam and I did dinner dishes: He washed, I dried. He taught me Punahou football songs, and we sang them loudly and happily—so much fun, I hated when the last dish was put away. Uncle Sam was spending his free time with University of Hawai'i friends. The cause of his previous shyness was gone; only faint scars remained on his face.

Within foster homes, I became self-reliant and able to bottle up emotions, because *behavior* matters in such an environment, not feelings. After experiencing openness and trust in rural Washington, I learned how suddenly all that can change, and I became wary and often quite afraid in metropolitan Los Angeles. Luckily, I left before serious harm was inflicted on me by a resentful, mean, older dull boy experiencing adolescent awakenings.

19. Ghost House

Outcomes of foster-home living were ingrained within my personality. I felt as a transient back in Hawai'i with phlegmatic grandparents. Grandpa wasn't as friendly as he once had seemed in letters. Grandma was remote. I didn't realize this had nothing to do with me—it was because of the ghosts I would learn about someday.

My jobs were to water plants and rake up blossoms dropping from flowering trees. Daily, except Sundays, I stuck a hose into almost a hundred anthurium pots adjacent to the house. Adjusting the hose nozzle, I fine-sprayed orchids in the glass hothouse Uncle Bob Lyman had built. It was next to two of his other creations: a goldfish pond and a Japanese garden surrounded by short, dense, spongy, sharp, itchy Japanese grass.

Mother said grandpa was a good father and also knew about raising troubled boys—although not suggesting I fit into that category. "His discipline will be good for you," she'd advised when turning me over as she headed first for the Island of Molokai. I followed Grandpa's written watering schedule for the three terraced acres, paying particular attention to plants producing fragrant flowers—gardenia, tuberose, pikake, ginger, and plumeria. These gave the yard a pleasant, rich aroma.

Grandpa believed he had one of Hawai'i's most diversified anthurium collections, as he propagated so many new varieties. I became exposed to flower sex education: spathes (male) and pistils (female) benignly participating in slow, passive reproduction. A giant poinciana tree and large golden and rainbow shower trees along the long, steep gravel driveway prevented direct sunlight from shining on them—anthuriums like the shade.

After moving in with my grandparents, I stopped wearing high-tops and went barefoot—even to school, as did other Island kids. Having flat feet, I started wearing such ungainly footwear for arch support when four years old. Now I could walk barefoot on sharp driveway stones without flinching; once I started doing that, Uncle Sam called me a *kama'āina*—a person belonging here. He tossed my ill-fitting high-tops into the trash.

A tightly trimmed, bright purple bougainvillea hedge arched over two stone columns at the property entrance. Uncle Sam climbed on a ladder to trim it. Grandpa used a push mower to cut the very nice front lawn. The rest of the terraced, densely planted property was all mine to rake and water. Being responsible for plants' well-being made barefoot me, now having cheek of tan, feel pretty darned important—I was the yardman!

I moved a water sprinkler around Grandpa's large vegetable garden, weeded spots where he couldn't hoe, and picked whatever was ripe. Although Grandpa looked big and powerful, tender knees prevented him from crawling under tomato plants and between rows of radishes, green onions, lettuce, and other edibles. It was up to smallish me to do that.

On moonlit nights, when mock orange shrubs or night-blooming cereus were ready to bloom, Grandma and Grandpa sat outside in reverent silence—watching the unfolding, savoring the aroma—the only ones in their quiet Eden.

The family's *Merriam-Webster Dictionary* sat on a stand in the alcove; next to it were a magnifying glass and a globe of the world. I cut the index cards Uncle Sam gave me into thirds, wrote new words on them, and placed the filled-out cards on my bedroom dresser for periodic review as I built a vocabulary. These were "flash cards": On one side was the word and on the other were associations. Uncle Sam taught me this technique while I was a beginning reader.

Experiences served as memory hooks. For instance, "benign" was Daddy Holzclaw smiling while explaining something in his fancy tongue-in-cheek language. "Imperious" was how Ma Holzclaw looked when she called me in from the Guinea fowl pen. "Benevolent" was her presenting Land of Oz books to me. "Ambivalence" was being with the Gulbransons. "Passivity" was living here.

I discovered that a large steamer trunk in my grandparents' underground red-dirt basement held *The Book of Knowledge.* Ten profusely illustrated, vividly written volumes were a treasure trove of information about the world and its famous people; they explained science, history, and fine art and gave instructions on things to make or do, contained music I could play on my violin, and explained literature and poetry. These books became my best friends.

I used editor Mees' comments about authors at school, speaking up, pretending that I was a literary expert on Clifton Fadiman's erudite *Information Please* radio show. I'd sit with Grandpa and listen to that show, sometimes knowing what they were discussing, thanks to eclectic reading and Uncle Sam's vocabulary boosting. Grandpa never acted surprised by what came out of my mouth. He was a big, quiet, dark man who gave me responsibilities. Uncle Belden said he once had a mischievous sense of humor, but it was gone.

Grandpa and Grandma drove over the Pali on Fridays so Maile could have an outing from the asylum. Grandma seemed agitated while preparing a picnic lunch in the morning, and Grandpa acted aloof. She appeared subdued when fixing a light supper in the evening; he looked forlorn. Friday was my day not to be obvious.

I went with them twice. Washed-out Aunt Maile spoke in a garbled way, saying, "I'm glad to see you" and "My, how you've grown." She repeated it several times, as if having nothing else to tell me.

She'd received a lobotomy. It's how the mental hospital treated schizophrenia.

She had called out and waved excitedly, years earlier, as I stood at the *Matsonia*'s rail when our journey to the West Coast was about to begin. That beautiful, spirited auntie was gone, replaced by a lifeless stranger.

Maile was my grandparents' only child known by a Hawaiian name. They probably realized very early that she wouldn't need to worry about assimilating.

I size things up quickly—it's a skill foster children acquire. That's how I knew ghosts of racial insecurity haunted my grandparents' home. Their quiet, subdued life was such a contrast to living among the convivial Holzclaws.

Washington-area neighbors arrived with beer, cheese, pickles, and—as Daddy liked to say—"The best of the wurst family." The family was made up of pork, beef, and veal sausages known as bockwurst, bratwurst, weinerwurst, weisswurst, and knockwurst.

Daddy Holzclaw loaded the kitchen stove with chunks of wood, started a fire, and placed sausages on the stovetop. They sizzled as they broiled. Neighbors gathered in the kitchen to drink beer; the grilling meat aroma tantalized and excited their appetites.

Adults lifted and clinked mugs and sang the German equivalent of "For He's a Jolly Good Fellow." It still rings in my head:

> Hoch soll sie leben,
> Hoch soll sie leben,
> Hoch soll sie leben,
> Dreimal hoch!

"Prosit!" Down-the-hatch! Refill mugs, clink, slug down more beer, chomp sausage, talk excitedly about any and everything, repeat the drinking song, continue the cycle—everyone's face becoming ruddy.

Once I had a tiny taste of Mount Rainier ale. "Why's it so tart?" I asked.

"The hops," Daddy Holzclaw said.

I stuck with Spezi: sweet-and-sour German-style lemonade mixed with root beer.

The Holzclaws and pals held large parties in a barn. Everyone went to a public park at the end of September for their Oktoberfest Festival.

Women wore colorful dirndl with puffed blouses, full skirts, and aprons. Ma Holzclaw explained: An apron knot on the left means the lady is single; if she had one on the right, she is married or "taken"; a knot on the back signified she's a widow.

Men wore short-sleeved shirts and lederhosen—black or green leather shorts, not quite reaching their knees, held up by suspenders. They had on long socks and half boots; a hat with a bright feather topped the costume. Boys wore scaled-down German lederhosen. I didn't have such an outfit, but being a blond, blue-eyed, excited six-year old, I didn't seem out of place among the Aryans.

They lived in Farm Country! Holzclaw neighbors brought what they grew, raised, smoked, and marinated—including hams, the wurst family, pigs' knuckles, hendl (chicken), sauerbraten, sauerkraut, and sour pickles.

You just don't know *how good* potato salad can be until you've had the vinegar-laced German style. It's true about their baked beans, too.

After everyone was satiated with bountiful German food, an accordionist began playing. Singing joyfully in German, men and women bounced up and down, danced, twirled, laughed, and perspired.

"Get out there and stomp around with widows," Ma directed, giving me a helpful little shove. More musicians arrived: trumpeter, baritone horn player, glockenspieler, and a bass drummer.

When musicians paused, men and women sang a four-word song: "Ein prosit der gemütlichkeit—Drink and to all good cheer," and waved their mugs. They sang it repeatedly. Everyone raised mugs during the last extended "gemütlichkeit" and punctuated the song with a hearty swallow. Throughout the afternoon and into the evening, someone was always breaking out into it. Of course, the crowd would join in, capping it with a rousing yell, "Prosit!"

Daddy Holzclaw was a patriotic American who'd fought for America against the Germans in World War I, but he never forgot his heritage. He sang "Deutschland über Alles," the crowd's last song, as loudly as everyone else:

> German women, German fidelity,
> German wine and German song.
> Deutsche Frauen, deutsche Treu
> Deutscher Wein und deutscher Sang.

Then earnest farm folk began cleaning everything up, packing garbage into gunnysacks to take home. "Little folk won't mess up the park by trolling through our trash," Daddy Holzclaw told me, with a wink, and went to work.

Sitting on a bench, I thought about trolls. Some have many heads, old ones are gruff and gnarled; if they've ever washed, it was long ago. Flies swarm around them, and weeds sprout from their noses and ears. Some trolls carry their heads under their arms. The hags have long, red, crooked noses. Trolls of all sizes come out at night to scavenge.

Hulder-people live under hills. Related to trolls in a garbled way, they also have no souls. Hulder-people look almost like human beings and send their bewitchingly beautiful hulder-maidens out at night. Each maiden keeps her long cow tail out of sight while attempting to lure a human boy into her power to take him to her underground world never to be seen again. But if a human can talk a hulder-maiden into marrying him in a Christian church, her tail will drop off and he will have a patient, hardworking wife.

While I daydreamed of trolls, Hulderfolk, and forest beings, the Germans neatly raked up all the scraps, leaving nothing for the supernatural to eat, and no left-behind mess to anger them.

Among the Gulbranson's Swedish cohorts, you helped yourself to whatever you wanted, wandered around, sat anywhere, ate as much as you were able, didn't have to mind your manners at a dining room table, and you were encouraged to continue helping yourself to more, more, and more!

Center of attention, the smorgasbord, was assembled from long boards placed on raised sawhorses. Women kept piling courses on it: hot and cold meat, smoked and pickled fish, salads, relishes, and never-ending scrumptious meatballs.

Men slugged down shots of vodka prefaced by a friendly "Skoal!" Actually, it was shots after shots. Chatter, chatter, chatter—not a somber, silent, cold-sober Swede in the house—except for "the designated drivers."

On Christmas Eve, the Gulbransons honored "Tomte," their "happiness spirit." This elf lived in their attic and brought good luck, said Mrs. Gulbranson. She hadn't actually seen him, but she knew what he looked like: "About your size—almost four feet—has a white beard, and often wears a red suit. Tomte, or Nisse, both his European names, became the model for the modern, universal Santa Claus," Mrs. Gulbranson said.

She fixed a bread pudding and left it out for him; we had some first to make sure it was sweet enough. Tomte emptied his pudding bowl while we slept and rewarded us with presents under the tree.

My favorite present, addressed "To Arthur from Aunt Eva," was a book of violin music including a solo variation of Elger's "Pomp and Circumstance." That music's ceremonial feeling stirred me when I heard the Los Angeles Philharmonic play it in the Hollywood Bowl. Aunt Eva, who took me, commented as I whistled some of it in the car, "You really liked that!"

Now I had real music for those opening notes: *Dee, dee-dee-dee, dee, dee . . .* all the best parts of the melody were scored for solo violin.

My life in Honolulu was in such sharp contrast: My grandparents' solemn home existence was punctuated by just three festive breaks: Thanksgiving, Christmas, and Easter. Each was like an extended church service.

Something had changed between Grandpa and me. He'd written chatty letters in beautiful script while I was at the Holzclaws and created appealing stories: One was about a lush fruit tree next to his driveway that on one Easter Day—and forever after—produced pink "strawberry" guavas instead of bigger yellow ones. He ended the story explaining how this pleased Grandma, who grew up enjoying freshly picked strawberries from her family's patch in Canada.

Grandpa didn't pay much attention to me now. He seemed serious, lost in thought, taciturn—almost as if he didn't know who I was, or who he was for that matter. I stopped hearing from him when in Los Angeles, but he did send a Christmas card with some money I used to buy lead soldiers.

No one ever visited them. I was curious about Hawaiian equivalents for prosit, skoal, wurst, and smorgasbord. I asked Uncle Sam why Grandpa didn't associate with people who looked like him.

"He's with lots of Hawaiians at Oʻahu Prison," he answered vaguely. "They call him 'Papa Lyman.' You see him dressed up and carrying his Hawaiian Bible and a flashlight every Tuesday evening, don't you? That's where he goes. He conducts Scripture lessons in Hawaiian for prisoners."

Is *that* where he expresses his heritage?

Grandpa was there when a Hawaiian was hung.

I figured that out: Hawaiians were hung on the nights Grandpa stayed at the prison until almost dawn. I heard him dragging his feet while passing through my bedroom to his; the next day the *Honolulu Star-Bulletin* reported, "Justice was done."

Hawaiian prisoners called Arthur's Grandpa "Poppa Lyman." He'd pray with them before they were hung.

Grandpa became moody. Having his own side of the house, he disappeared in there for a couple days, coming out only to fix a snack in the kitchen, returning without saying anything. Grandma and I had supper together without him.

She lived on the other side of the house and had her own bedroom, bathroom, and a bathtub. Sometimes, for a treat, she let me soak in bubble bath in her tub. I had to take a shower first in another part of the house if I'd been digging in the garden.

Grandpa and I went to the Kaimukī grocery store, where I saw intriguing foods from many cultures: Chinese, Japanese, Korean, Filipino, and Portuguese. Except for Grandpa's sparse weekly treats, neither foods nor people of other cultures came to the home—except for the Chinese vegetable man.

He arrived Saturdays at about 2:00 p.m. I looked forward to hearing his melodic singsong message: "I got special California pineapple today!" It meant he was hawking artichokes. They don't really look like pineapples, but a guttural "Aka-cho-ka" lacks an appealing Chinese tone, so he concocted that description after Grandma told him I learned to love artichokes while in California. She always bought "California pineapples" whenever the Chinaman sang. Grandma was always a good customer for strawberries and fruits and vegetables not grown in our garden.

His vehicle had a front cab for the driver; the rest of the open truck held rows of open boxes holding vegetables and fruit. Vegetables hung on the truck's top and sides. Uncle Belden said his truck looked like a moving forest, "The way Malcolm and Macduff disguised their armies in Shakespeare's *Macbeth*." Mr. Chinaman maneuvered in low gear up our steep driveway, ringing his bell: "Ting-ting-ting-a-ling."

Grandpa chatted with the grocery store's butcher who sliced *poke*—raw fish and raw liver that Grandpa savored. He ate those Hawaiian tidbits at supper on shopping day. Grandma went "tsk-tsk" when he offered me a taste from his side of the table. I pretended to enjoy whatever he gave me—"We were being men together."

Their "boys," Sam and brothers Belden and Bob, joined us for Thanksgiving and Christmas dinners. These were preceded by a family worship service—Bible readings and prayers. I'd be asked to sing the first verse of a hymn.

Formal holiday meals at the dining table were quiet, bland, and always the same: a roast chicken or a turkey, mashed things (sweet and regular potatoes and squash), giblet gravy, peas, and a fruit salad made with Jell-O. On Thanksgiving we had pumpkin pie; on Christmas, mincemeat pie with a side of sugary hard sauce—plain vanilla, no rum flavoring, this being "A House of Temperance" (Grandma's words).

My palate had been stimulated by the Holzclaws' and Gulbransons' ethnic treats. My taste buds were sedated by Grandma's bland, New England–style missionary food.

After graduating from the University of Hawai'i, Uncle Sam joined the army because of what Germany was doing. He was stationed at Schofield Barracks.

Grandma and I didn't sing while doing dishes. Although not usually talkative, she'd sometimes describe her girlhood in British Columbia. Grandma had "commemorative teaspoons" honoring British kings and queens that she "began saving when a girl." She seemed "ved-dy" British when describing royalty and high tea. I may have inherited her collecting propensity—my stamps and lead soldiers, you know.

A pleasant Japanese boy my age lived about a block away. We saw each other Sundays, the day I didn't water. Grandpa wasn't happy about our friendship. Innocently, I'd told Grandpa my friend's father bought cases of canned food, in case of a storm. The two of us had stacked cans on shelves in their cement basement; his father fixed Japanese noodles and charcoaled strips of steak as our reward.

"They are stockpiling," Grandpa growled angrily.

Uncle Sam had explained that Grandpa had bitter feelings after "The Sack of Nanking" appeared in a 1938 issue of the *Reader's Digest* magazine. It described horrors when the Japanese army invaded that Chinese city.

I had to snub my only close friend because of something that happened in another part of the world.

By now I'd completed all I chose to read within *The Book of Knowledge*. Editor Arthur Mees interpreted Tennyson's Lotus-Eaters "as living apathetically." If not for the nearby branch library, I would've experienced similar torpor from tedious spading, watering, raking, and loneliness when not in school.

There was no hostility in the house—just polite avoidance. Uncle Belden said Grandma used to be very bossy to Grandpa. "One night he brought a pair of his overalls to the dining room table—there were too many of us to eat in the kitchen in those days. Thinking he'd brought them to be mended, Mother said: 'Put them in my sewing room and I'll take care of them.' Dad replied, 'These don't need mending. They're now yours to wear.' Mother asked, 'What? Why?' Dad replied, 'You act so bossy. It's as if you wear the pants in this family. So I brought you these. If you want to be The Boss of the House, you'd better put 'em on!' Her face turned red. From then on, I don't ever remember Mother giving Dad orders in front of us."

I said, "They act subdued around me."

"Something terrible broke their spirit," Uncle Belden responded vaguely.

While being in the foster home system, I learned to keep my mouth shut and follow the "Be seen but not heard" adage. Belden's sad expression made me realize this was not a time to ask for an explanation.

Knowing about picking up a conversation by changing the subject, I shared a personal experience: "Grandpa recently taught me two new words: *Initiative* is what you are supposed to do, *insubordination* is what you must never do."

"Please, some background," responded Uncle Belden.

"Well, Grandpa prepared my raking schedule. I followed it faithfully until it got me into trouble. *Initiative*— lack of it in this case— was my not *immediately* raking up all the poinciana blossoms a heavy wind dumped on the driveway. I wasn't scheduled to do that job until a day later. 'Do work when it needs to be done. Don't hide behind a schedule,' he lectured.

"*Insubordination* was a more severe offense—it got me whipped.

"I'd snuck out to play football on a Sunday. Grandpa and Grandma call Sunday 'The Lord's Day of Rest,' as you know. When he learned I was playing instead, Grandpa cut a bamboo stick from a bush in our backyard. He made me bend over and grab my ankles, and he whipped me with the stick several times. He yelled out *"Insubordination!"* before each swing so I'd make the connection.

"Learning that word stung, but I didn't show tears. The Lord had punished me already. Tackled hard when carrying the football, I chipped a front tooth on the in-ground water sprinkler in the backyard where we played."

"Dad is stern," Uncle Belden remarked, and then he told me about his own disciplinary experience when he was a teenager.

"He'd smelled cigarette smoke on my breath. The next day, your grandfather made me sit down and smoke a big, wicked-tasting cigar until I threw up. Haven't smoked since."

20. Bookishly Brave

I sped through many of the Kaimukī branch library's youthful reading selections.

A kindly librarian suggested other books and ordered them from the downtown main library. She allowed me to continue renewing some until I'd almost committed them to memory.

Two became part of my life: *The Boy's King Arthur,* adapted by Sidney Lanier from Thomas Mallory's original book, with art by N. C. Wyeth; and *The Merry Adventures of Robin Hood,* with writing and drawings by Howard Pyle, greatest illustrator of his day.

Reading experiences became locked within my consciousness and formed lasting impressions. I always remembered what Ma Holzclaw had told me about how artists' draw to expand your mind. Pyle's and Wyeth's realism stimulated my mental imagery with their portrayal of human emotions, action, tension, shadows, vibrant colors, and enchantment. My "spiritual eye" sometimes made things in real life appear as if painted by them. I experienced a transition between two worlds whenever this occurred.

My associations with King Arthur's knights and Robin Hood began when I was almost nine years old. Acting out their adventures, speaking for all characters, I uttered rousing perorations, waved my sword with companion knights, and joined the Merry Men in shooting arrows at the corrupt Sheriff of Nottingham and his skulking cohorts.

Grandpa was about six feet tall and weighed over 250 pounds. His discarded undershirt became a wonderful flowing floor-length cape. A metal garbage can cover with a handy handle was my shield. The backyard's bamboo bushes provided lance, sword, bow, and arrows.

I was shoeless but formidable, no longer had a hacking asthmatic cough, and my imagination just flowed.

The bamboo sword broke while I fought a Druid disguised as a *wiliwili* tree that had dropped pods to blind me, and now he wanted to cut off my head so I'd be a human sacrifice. Trustworthy Sir Gawain said, "Don't worry."

He stepped in against Celtic warriors waving iron swords who appeared from behind the Druid. Battling furiously, Sir Gawain struck them down, had them all plead for mercy, and made the Druid priest promise not to involve me in his grisly religious practices. Good guy Gawain released them. The tree stopped shedding pods on me.

After that, I kept my eyes alert while passing rice paddies and duck ponds near Waikīkī, hoping the Lady of the Lake's hand would rise to offer me Excalibur. It materialized in Grandpa's garage, lying on a shelf next to his Ford automobile, disguised as a metal strip. I imagined having Siegfried's magic and believed it was now a perfect knightly weapon.

Merlin's spell stopped the bleeding when Excalibur was knocked from my hand in battle. The scar's on my left index finger.

Uncle Sam had lost part of his left ring finger when he was thirteen years old and "fooling around on the wire fence"—those are Grandma's exact words. A lush Mauna Loa vine with blood-red blooms now flourished on that backyard fence, probably nourished by my uncle's missing part.

I kept my cut secret—otherwise, Grandma would've confiscated magnificent Excalibur, demeaning that noble weapon, calling it "Arthur's fooling-around piece of metal."

Grandma was a kindly, quiet, uncomplicated lady with a strong will who could be very direct. Guess that's why Grandpa offered her his work pants. One night while we did dishes together, I told her I was reading Sir Walter Scott's *Border Minstrelsy*. "Archie and Johnny Armstrong are in it. When Archie was a jester in the English Court, he knew Sir John Falstaff."

Both Armstrongs were rogues, something I didn't mention.

I did tell her about invaders attacking a Scottish castle that seemed doomed to fall and recited these lines from the book: "A lookout from the castle walls saw a group of warriors coming to rescue them. The king asked, 'Be they Christians?' The watchman said, 'Nae, they be Armstrongs. And mighty they be.'"

Grandma didn't like that humor. I tried explaining: "It's Scott's wordplay. 'Christian' and 'Armstrong' are two families' surnames."

She wanted me to realize that *Armstrongs* have always been firm Christians, that Scott was leading me astray, and that he was no "Sir"; Armstrong was her maiden name. I stopped giving book reports.

About a week later, she presented me with a book of Christian children's stories and said, "These are more suitable for your age."

Chronological age, yes, not reading-level age; Dear Grandma, we were on different wavelengths.

Uncle Sam continued encouraging me: "Reading will expand your mind and vocabulary," he'd say and would ask to see my flash cards. He'd nod approvingly at the growing stack.

Realizing I really worked at this, he told me to let him know when I needed more card stock.

Nineteenth-century adventure writers gave my mind all the stimulation it craved; I used large words and archaic expressions profusely—including "forsooth, swoon, swain," and "smote." And I always said "surely."

Adults who didn't know about me looked puzzled when hearing me speak.

Never did I disclose my secret life in Camelot and Sherwood Forest—not even to Uncle Sam. He probably knew.

A few blocks away, a boy with polio lived in an iron lung. Following the Golden Rule, "Do unto others as has been done to you," I went to see him, a book in hand. Two or three afternoons a week I acted out stories, sitting on the floor below Alfredo. Looking down, he watched my facial expressions intensely. I was being an actor—just like my hero Frank Baum.

We'd finished Stevenson's *Treasure Island* and were coming to the part in Defoe's *Robinson Crusoe* about Crusoe and Friday beating off the cannibals. While walking home, I gnashed my teeth and practiced savage screams for tomorrow's reading.

An ambulance took Alfredo to Queen's Hospital that night. He didn't return.

21. War Tremors

News reached me that Grandma told her adult Sunday school Class students I was a peaceful and mild little boy—a "grand grandchild."

That's because no one knew how I behaved in imaginary life. When creative energies boil, I become a knight-errant who uses a battle-ax to chop at—and even behead—any foe!

Evil villains, disguised as garden dirt, stand no chance against mighty me with battle-ax-hoe in hand.

When watering plants on terraces, my "inner eyes" are often stimulated by dark shadows within hanging stephanotis.

And to the right—among the ylang-ylang vines, clustering amongst big-leaved philodendron—what might be hiding there?

Sunlight shining through the hose's fine spray creates a light rainbow diffusing into imagery. Gazing through, I see beautiful maidens surrounding Arthur, the once and future king. He is sleeping in the fairy isle of Avalon, waiting for the day when his people will call for him again.

Loneliness and a growing sense of individuality stimulated fantasies beyond those arising from the pages of library books. Books were conduits to creativeness; I was ready to enter my own world—instead of just playing out what others had described.

My grandparents gave up trying to augment my avid reading with Christian children's books. Those were childish for me; I tried delving into the Bible, beginning with "The Begats," attempting to read the stories. Familiarity, but very little fascination, was all that I gained at that point. I wouldn't be intrigued by the evil Whore of Babylon until I saw her—over ten feet tall and in living color!

Except for Friday visits to Aunt Maile, Grandpa spent weekday mornings reading and writing in his Scofield Study Bible. "One day, when I am through with it, you can have it," he said. "It contains daily thoughts."

I'll be an old man before learning what is on his mind.

He took me to an evening meeting at McKinley High School, home of Honolulu's largest auditorium. We went to learn about the book of Revelation. A renowned lecturer from the mainland was here for a revival meeting. He used lanternslides to dramatize his basic message: "The world is heading to total destruction." This was 1938: His prediction was on target.

The speaker reviewed and praised the life of John Knox, a converted Roman Catholic, who focused on Revelation. Knox was a contemporary of John Calvin, whose doctrine was embedded within many of Hawai'i's early missionaries. Grandpa was a strict Calvinist. This was the first time I'd heard anyone explain the doctrine Grandpa followed, which he often expressed in terms of "You must," or "It's forbidden." Because he referred to fairies as "Fallen Angels," I didn't discuss fairy lore I'd read—even though he wrote about his guava bush magically producing strawberry instead of yellow guavas.

Hollywood had begun releasing movies in color. After *The Mikado* and *The Wizard of Oz,* I thought I was accustomed to visual excitement.

But I was shocked here by seeing the end of the world startlingly projected on a huge screen. Surrealistic artwork and ghoulish oversized images had a science-fiction fascination. The painted-up Whore of Babylon resembled a horrible troll. The speaker and his images scared the hell out of me. I guess that was the point.

"Armageddon is upon us," declared the speaker. He held up a Bible and asserted, "All is described in here!"

As we drove home, I told Grandpa I wasn't ready for the book of Revelation.

"You will be someday," he promised.

I'd returned to Hawai'i in 1938; war hadn't begun in Europe, but undercurrents were strong. Residents discussed Hawai'i's vulnerability, isolated in the middle of the Pacific.

Before a Saturday dinner at my grandparents, my three uncles discussed changes in Mānoa. That cool scenic area was a residential enclave for well-to-do Caucasians.

Belden said, "Well-to-do Chinese—I'm being redundant—are buying Mānoa homes. It's the first time they've had this chance. Haole, leaving because of the war scare, are selling to Pake, who are the only ones willing to pay what sellers ask."

Uncle Bob joined in: "Mary confided that her family will be moving to Iowa, smack dab in the middle of America. She explained, 'Father wants us away from East and West Coasts because he says they'll be vulnerable.'" Mary, his contemporary, is a "cousin," the term Hawai'i's original missionary family descendants' use for one another.

Uncle Sam later explained that such thinking began spreading after Hitler came to power: "Americans are afraid of Hitler."

Punahou schoolmates repeated what parents said about the Depression, Roosevelt, our country's vulnerability, and Hawai'i's isolation. One kid that I tried to avoid came up to me and said in his whiny nyah-nyah voice, "I'm moving to the mainland to live with my grandparents. I'll be safe with them while you're blitzed with yours!"

I may have been the only one in school who didn't reside with parents. I interpreted his comment as meaning that he no longer thought my living with grandparents was "abnormal."

Radio stations KGU and KGMB fed the outside world to us. Along with millions of Americans, Grandpa and I listened weekly to Father Charles Coughlin. Two famous Americans also came on the air with him: Charles A. Lindbergh and Henry Ford thought "Jews were trying to drive America into war and we should ally ourselves with Hitler before it is too late." Lindbergh respected Germans for their large, modern air force and sense of national purpose; Ford praised Germany's industrial mass production and work ethos.

Coughlin was a Michigan Catholic priest who believed that neither capitalism, democracy, nor Franklin D. Roosevelt's policies had a future. Uncle Belden told me Father Coughlin might be a Nazi.

The U.S. Office of War Information countered with its own radio series, *You Can't Do Business with Hitler.* Its speakers were insipid and stagy in contrast with the fiery Father Coughlin.

Father Coughlin made it obvious the world was changing. In 1938, Czech residents welcomed Hitler's troops marching into Czechoslovakia's Sudetenland. He reported that banners were raised proclaiming "One Folk, One Reich, One Führer." It was the beginning of Hitler's mastery of Europe, and the German army poured over the Polish border, rolled over the Netherlands and France, and was now preparing to invade Britain.

Grandpa listened and muttered. Within earshot, Grandma and I sat in the alcove playing Chinese checkers and regular checkers. She was a whiz at both. Neither board games with dice nor playing cards were allowed in their house—those were like gambling.

Checkers didn't involve any of the Devil's devices and were okay.

People don't always explain to children enough about what's going on. One night, when a cigarette commercial interrupted Father Coughlin, I asked: "Grandpa, kids in school are leaving Hawai'i with their families. Does that have anything to do with what we're hearing on the radio?"

He gave me a straightforward but unusually eloquent answer: "Hawai'i is a fragile place to be, considering all that's happening on the world stage. Hitler's march through Europe is terrifying. The world is changing. That's why people are leaving for the mainland."

This was clear: Hitler was like Mordred, who had used his own types of Nazis to destroy King Arthur's tranquil Camelot.

Grandpa became an American Red Cross volunteer in 1940 and taught first aid at about the same time my uncles entered military service. I nodded respectfully when seeing him in his Red Cross uniform: khaki trousers and khaki shirt, white armband with a red cross, metal helmet on his head, whistle on a loop around his neck. Wearing a white dress, Grandma went along to "roll bandages." She, too, wore a Red Cross armband.

At home she knitted wool socks for the English, "Because cold weather is coming and Germans are bombing Londoners out of their homes."

"**U.S.** Freezes Japanese Assets," read the *Honolulu Star-Bulletin*'s" front-page headline on Friday, December 5, 1941.

Standing and holding on to the trolley strap, riding home from Punahou School, I squinted down on the newspaper article a seated man was reading. When he looked up, I asked what the headline meant.

"We're keeping Japan's money," he said.

That next day's paper published the photograph of a sentry guarding a local reservoir. The caption explained: "This is a precaution due to unrest between Japan and America. The soldier is safeguarding a valuable water source from poisoning by retaliatory spies."

My uncles were with us for the weekend. On Sunday morning, around 9:00 a.m., they brewed Kona coffee my mother sent and listened to recorded symphonic music on KGU. Ready for Sunday school, I sat with them while Grandpa and Grandma finished dressing.

They looked up in surprise as the studio announcer broke in to say, "One moment please." Then a radio newsman on the roof of the *Honolulu Advertiser*'s newspaper building told us, "Pearl Harbor is being bombed by Japanese planes, and the city of Honolulu has been attacked. There is no doubt that this is a real war."

The stern-sounding studio announcer cut in and restated, "This is a real war!"

My uncles returned immediately to their bases. Grandpa adamantly declared, "We *are going* to Sunday school!"

I later learned that Uncle Bob, a navy submariner, did "body detail" at Pearl Harbor.

Some weeks later the *War Cry,* the Salvation Army's national publication, wanted to send a photographer to my grandparents' home for a story about "Patriotism." The person who phoned explained their story angle to Grandma: "Retired Majors Lyman have three sons serving their country and both are Red Cross volunteers."

During supper, Grandma told Grandpa, "They want to write about the boys, describe what you do, and will mention my rolling bandages and knitting wool socks for Bundles for Britain."

Grandpa was against it. He absolutely refused to allow the *War Cry* to include them both in a picture.

Taking it all in, I read between the lines: Grandpa didn't want his and Grandma's contrasting skin colors displayed to the Salvation Army world.

Ghosts haunted their home.

I was unaware of the hurt he experienced when the commander in California had described him as "That big, dark man who is courting red-haired Charlotte Armstrong." Leaders were required to marry only from within the Salvation Army; a potential mixed marriage must have been "radical" during the early days when my grandparents enlisted.

The commander shipped Grandpa to England to serve under General Booth, the Salvation Army's founder.

After successfully preaching in London, first as a curiosity and then as a celebrity, "Hallelujah the Hawaiian" returned to California and married "the Tall Canadian."

They were stationed in Washington State and my mother was born there. The Salvation Army transferred them to the Big Island, Hawai'i, and five more Lyman babies arrived, including "Evangeline," named after General Booth's daughter. Aunt Eva was one of General Booth's godchildren.

I once proudly told one of our Punahou teachers about Aunt Eva being General Booth's Godchild. In a very uppity tone, she replied, "Do you realize *how many* Godchildren General Booth must have?"

"No," I answered. "But how do any others *diminish* Aunt Eva?"

Diminish: That innocent repartee made her sputter.

Uncle Sam had an adage for me to follow: "Always say things right: It'll amaze your friends and confound your adversaries." He modified a Mark Twain saying to encourage me to become a wordsmith.

I was learning to stand my own ground politely after passing the biblical phase of "When I was a child

I spoke as a child, I understood as a child." Reading, vocabulary boosting, and wariness surfaced in what I said and understood.

Grandpa and Grandma reported to the Kaimukī Red Cross shelter during the week. They jointly taught Sunday school to adults at a community church. He continued going to jail on Tuesdays and inspected my outdoor work every few days or so. Grandpa was glad we'd enlarged the garden and spoke of growing some rows of sweet corn.

Both attended services downtown at the Salvation Army Citadel on Sunday afternoons and both taught morning Sunday school in Kaimukī.

I've mentioned Grandpa being a big man. He looked majestic in his black officer's uniform with its "Blood and Fire" crest, with a military-styled officer's hat on his thick white hair. My tall Grandma laced herself up in a corset that accentuated her always-erect posture. She wore her waist-length white hair in a bun. Grandma was imposing in her full-length black lassie dress and black poke bonnet.

These two Salvationists must have created a memorable appearance when exiting their large, black, four-door Ford sedan and striding into the Citadel.

Internal conflicts and racial stings caused Majors Charlotte and David Lyman to retire early from the Salvation Army and the Kaimukī Boys Home they had founded. I didn't know the details—Uncle Belden had hinted at something, and I formed my own conclusions: Grandpa might have been too strict.

I hadn't discovered how far children are able to go despite adult-imposed handicaps and indifference. I didn't know that a child can lead. I was unaware of my potential to banish ghosts. I simply read, existed within a fantasy world, did what I was supposed to do, and tried staying out of the way. My grandparents probably believed I still thought as a child.

Grandpa bought a Mother' Service Banner for Grandma and hung it on the living room window overlooking the driveway. It was rectangular, about eight by fourteen inches, with three blue stars on a white field sewn on a red banner.

I wanted the *War Cry* to recognize "The Patriotic Lymans." Grandpa didn't realize how relentless quiet me could be. I brought up the subject during dinnertime at the kitchen table, beginning with a bland statement: "You certainly can be proud your three sons *volunteered* to serve our country."

When I said that, Grandpa stopped eating for a moment, looking up warily.

He didn't answer and resumed enjoying his fresh *poke;* it'd been his day for grocery shopping. After he'd finished his treat, I spoke up again: "I'll bet a 'Three-Star Family' like ours is unusual. We're maybe even inspiring. If more people knew about our work on the Home Front they might want to be War Volunteers too."

I'd switched speaking style from second person to first person plural, having learned about bringing collective nouns into conversation from reading Booth Tarkington's *Penrod* book. That clever twelve-year-old's convincing way of talking kept him steps ahead of most adults. I practiced imitating Penrod, and this was a chance to apply what I'd learned.

Grandma smiled but said nothing. Grandpa appeared to reflect momentarily, then piled potatoes and gravy onto his plate. He loved to eat.

During supper the next night, I tried another approach: "Your Mother's Service Banner is like an emblem of honor, isn't it, Grandma? If we lived on a main road, more people would see it and know about you and your sons." I knew how to use young Penrod's obliqueness.

Since we were on a hillside, only the mailman, paperboy, and an occasional meter reader saw the Banner. The Chinese vegetable man looked straight ahead while driving to the back door.

Grandma's honor was the deciding shot among my dinnertime salvos. Grandpa said he'd talk to the *War Cry* reporter. The photo was taken of them in civilian clothes—not in their Salvation Army uniforms.

I'm certain they prayed daily they wouldn't have to replace a blue star with the gold symbol of a fallen warrior. After Christmas I was sent to live with my mother to escape heavy fighting expected during Japan's imminent invasion of O'ahu.

Grandma and Grandpa, "The Patriotic Lymans," photographed for The Salvation Army "War Cry" *publication.*

22. A Place for Us

Mother didn't receive child support from my dad, wherever he was. I knew nothing about him. She helped pay for me, whenever she had a job; otherwise charity filled the void. The state reimbursed my foster parents. I realized that living with my grandparents was a financial hardship for them when Mother was between jobs. It's why I was proud of my yardman status.

Mother's new "job package" included housing in the former nurses' quarters at the abandoned Kona Hospital on the Big Island of Hawai'i. It had a room for me. We were the only persons in that vast hospital complex. This was a chance to know her.

She'd worked previously in San Luis Obispo, California, an agricultural region, and told me about it: "Agriculture attracted many of the 250,000 persons who moved to California in the mid-1930s," she explained. "Most were Oklahoma tenant farmers escaping 'the Dust Bowl'—the drought caused farms to fail."

Mother was in California when police established a "bum blockade" at the state's border to keep out the

Okies. She dealt with transients similar to folks James Steinbeck described in his book *The Grapes of Wrath*. She used my father's surname "Rath" so it wouldn't be different from mine. People who'd heard of the book thought she wrote it.

"Many were just backward and overwhelmed," she explained.

I visited her once and stayed at a hotel in Atascadero, in the artichoke heartland.

Before I moved to a California foster home, Ma Holzclaw had taught me to sing in public. Mother had me perform at a Salvation Army service.

The hotel's head bellman loaned me a scaled-down uniform, and I resembled four-foot-tall Johnnie the Bellhop, whose piercing high-pitched (B-flat) voice—"Call for Phillip Mor-rees"—was broadcast on radio networks.

Dressed to sing a solo at a California Salvation Army service, Arthur wears a uniform concocted by a hotel bellman.

In Kona, Mother explained about Ignacy Jan Paderewski, the world-famous pianist who came to Paso Robles in San Luis Obispo County to have his arthritis treated at its thermal mineral springs. His family, once prosperous landowners, were deprived of their property in Poland. Paderewski decided to reestablish the family's farming tradition in America—the land of new opportunity. He purchased 1,520 San Luis Obispo acres and started growing high-quality almonds and grapes imported from Europe. He'd added 4,000 more acres when Mother met him.

The maestro urged Mother to keep her eyes open for transient families with children; he felt these persons had the greatest need to work. She drove them to Paderewski's orchards for an interview. Those who were given jobs and their families were transported by a police van to unlocked jail cells. These served as their temporary housing. "Jails were clean, safe places, and the county delivered healthy meals," she explained.

"Paderewski built housing for his workers; they loved him very much."

After reading *The Grapes of Wrath*, I realized that Mother provided a form of *social justice*. Maybe I'd gained this perspective from listening to Ma Holzclaw describe "Doc R's" helping people get back on their feet. Grandpa was a Republican, as were most old-time Hawaiian residents, and he was less praiseworthy of FDR.

Mother told me that the Holzclaws, childless because of Daddy's World War I injuries, wanted to adopt me. She thought I would have a very good life there. For some reason, Grandpa was against it, and Mother did what he said. I went to the foster home in Los Angeles—and now, at age nine, I live with Mother.

Acres of wild guava bushes behind the hospital yielded juicy yellow fruit with pink insides. Mother said they grew for me to pick, scrub, slice, bag, and smash.

Mother bought our poi in cloth bags that she washed and saved for me to fill with a guava mess that'd hang in our kitchen jelly factory. Pectin-packed aromatic juice dripped from bags into pots. Adding sugar, mother poured the boiled mixture into sterilized jars for cooling, setting, and sealing with wax. This entire fascinating process seemed magical.

Sweets were rare during the war. The gift jars of reddish jelly she carried in her briefcase were probably a big hit with welfare clients. I assume so; she didn't talk about it.

I learned how closely Mother identified with Hawaiians. Those on relief, on a ranch, on a fishing boat, and members of the Kailua, Miloli'i, Puna, and Keaukaha clans we associated with were considered "family." Going to a luau was the equivalent of a party with Holzclaw cohorts.

Ruth Hualani Lyman Rath traveled the Island of Hawai'i's 4,038 square miles. Covering that area—at thirty miles an hour top highway speed and with wartime restrictions on nighttime driving—meant I was often home alone. That was okay with me: By age nine I could fend for myself. Books and a lively imagination kept loneliness away; on clear nights, Mother Nature provided thrilling, although scary, spectacles.

Our hilltop porch looked westward toward the ocean. Sunset began with subtle color changes as the bright-red sun—seemingly—moved from high in the sky down to deep in the ocean. When the sun "sank," the blue sea turned fiery red and glowed. Sea and sky quickly became black, black, black!

This finale evoked a visceral reaction. It was similar to how I'd felt while reading H. G. Wells' *The War of the Worlds*—scary but fascinating. One of his lines seemed to describe Kona sunsets:

> The sudden change of a sunny landscape,
> Threads of red fire,
> Dark shadows on the green treetops,
> Black smoke that hides everything.

Wells wrote about invading Martians—might this happen in isolated Kona?

Konawaena School was three miles away. I walked alone and had no after-school companions because no one lived near Hospital Hill. Students, predominately Japanese children from small coffee farms, were very different from Punahou's excitable chatterboxes.

They sat stoically through high school basketball games. Should one of our team's players steal the ball, make a fast break, and score, there would be dead silence. Games in the gym could have been church services—except those would've included singing.

Konawaena students behaved similarly in the classroom. Most did very good schoolwork, but they were reared to observe, absorb, and not say much. These were taciturn, humble, earnest, and exceedingly polite students. Never once did I hear "Nyah-nyah" during my three years at serious Konawaena.

23. I Discover Me

I felt isolated until discovering my identity sat on a shelf in Mother's storage room.

First clues to follow were in Mother's book about Hilo Boarding School written by Sarah Joiner Lyman; she and David Belden Lyman, her husband, founded the school. Grandpa was named after his grandfather, the school's founder; his Hawaiian mother's name gave him Kuana for a middle name, meaning "first position" or "standing"—suitable for an elder boy of fifteen children, don't you think?

I found information about the famous Hawaiian king from whom Grandpa's mother, Hualani, descended. Details were on a chronology chart Mother updated in her funny penmanship. My name was listed as Kuali'i's 135th descendent—me, myself, and I, who'd arrived in Kona with waiflike insecurity after a transient life. All those relatives listed in these books represented identity— maybe even some stability. Despite his looks, Grandpa never mentioned a word about his Hawaiian lineage.

I grasped so eagerly at these roots. "Hualani," grandfather's mother's name, means "offspring of a chief"—a chief with an extraordinary history, I was discovering. Hualani was also my mother's Hawaiian name. Grandpa must've wanted to carry it on at the time my mother was born.

I was a young tendril, craving something to cling to, wanting to grow strong and proud in the sunlight—instead of being weak and unnoticed in the dark. I'd never lived in one place more than two years; every move meant adapting to others' idiosyncrasies. Living that way made me feel cast off—being the me nobody knows.

I was intensely curious about the Lyman potpourri. Withdrawn grandfather had shared nothing. Sarah Joiner Lyman, an original missionary ancestor, wrote about everything, and Mother continued Sarah Lyman's genealogical recordkeeping without sharing it; Grandpa's phobia made his children closeted Hawaiians.

The nearby Kealakekua branch library included books by writers who'd stayed in the Lyman family's home and school when Hilo had no hotel. It was the community's cultural center, and Grandpa grew up nearby. Mother's recordkeeping showed Grandpa's father, Rufus Anderson Lyman, was a circuit judge, lieutenant governor, and business advisor to the royal governor, Princess Ruth Ke'elikōlani. He'd helped Princess Ruth own the most land in the Islands. Rufus wrote a biography of his close friend Kamehameha V—King Lot—the last of that ruling line of the blood. My mother's Christian name "Ruth" was in honor of Princess Ruth.

I was blessed to know all this because of my mother, a Hawaiian bibliophile. (I don't think she knew I was devouring her books.)

I read books written by Lyman's guests: Herman Melville, 1841, Samuel Clements (Mark Twain) 1866, Jack London, 1902. Robert Louis Stevenson, the Lyman's 1889 guest, was the very person who first helped me to feel better about myself!

I sought firsthand information, beginning with Aunty Kalei Lyman, Grandpa's sister-in-law, whose late husband Clarence was one of three Lyman brothers to overcome racial barriers and graduate from the United States Military Academy at West Point.

Grandpa's brothers with Hawai'i's queens. Left to right, Charles Reed Bishop Lyman (West Point 1913 #55188, became Brig. General); Queen Kapiolani; Queen Lili'uokalani; Albert Kuali'i Brickwood Lyman (West Point 1909 #4764, became Brig. General). Elder brother First Lieutenant Clarence Kumukoa Lyman (West Point 1905 #4382) died during World War I.

Concentrating on "perspective" as well as going to school meant no traveling.

I went to the eucalyptus tree now and then to tell Kahu what I was doing and to learn what's happening on Menehune Plains. He reported: "Ah Soong and Miki have been going to old menehune fishponds on Lyman land in Puna. 'Ōpelu have fattened; Miki, a really good spear fisherman, dove in and brought out lots of fish for Ah Soong to season and dry. They saved the fattest for a huge fish fry; menehune women ate with the men.

"Miki bragged about menehune being more civilized than Hawaiians in this and other regards."

"Rising Sun's sulking since you've stopped appearing; no one wants to listen to his bragging about Japan's military.

"Per'fesser brought Aiko to visit Queen Esther, her gown designer. Aiko and the Per'fesser snip material from Honolulu's Liberty House at night, always leaving an envelope containing money by the cash register."

"Menehune borrow, they don't steal," Kahu states.

"Queen Esther is planning her annual ceremonial pilgrimage to 'Sacred Sandalwood Groves.' Some of her court accompany her for solace.

"Are you almost finished reflecting?"

"Yes," I answered. "Have you planned some trips?"

Kahu nodded vigorously, then went into the guava bushes.

Now! I've finished writing remembrances of things past; my personal story has been placed into *perspective*. I'm ready to travel and to tell Per'fesser that I wrote my history just as he said I should.

24. Hip-Hip Hooray/ USA!

Early the next morning, hearing big vehicles driving up Hospital Hill in low gear, I walk out to the front porch to see what is going on, being unable to gaze out of our wartime "blackout" painted windows. Not to worry; an American star is painted on each olive-drab truck.

They park, and soldiers climb out.

Huge tents rise. I walk over to greet the new neighbors. A guidon hanging from a truck identifies them as members of the 27th Division National Guard from New York State. Wandering around, I say "Howzit!" and wave to anyone looking in my direction.

A captain asks if I know my way around the hills behind the hospital. I nod eagerly and lead him and half a dozen soldiers through the heavy brush, staying away from the zigzag passageway to Shangri-La.

The captain wants sites for artillery guns. Discovering we're too distant from potential landing areas—being seven miles from Kealakekua Bay—he gives up that idea.

He is pleased when I show him the large roofed-in area back of the hospital where an ambulance was once "garaged."

Some army men carry in cooking supplies and make that place into a mess hall. The head cook and his assistant are of Italian ancestry; I accept their invitation to "chow down"—his words—the next time he prepares spaghetti and meatballs. He says to "show up" when he fixes something called lasagna. "It'll put some meat on your bones," he explains.

Soldiers build showers next to hospital water tanks and install latrines and outhouses where they can dig through loose lava.

A few days later, I am thrilled to see a gun barrel sticking out of my "invisible" little fort on Hospital Hill. Rising Sun sneered and said, "My preparations were useless." Ha!

I created a bona fide machine gun nest.

Details are hazy. Everything happens so quickly while Hospital Hill converts into an army base. Mother says, "Stay away from the soldiers." She doesn't, though. A military policeman from Texas has become her friend.

Soldiers teach me to shoot on the shooting range they've built not far from a little building Mother calls her office. One soldier opens his footlocker, shows me a tommy gun, and says, "This is like the submachine guns British commandos use."

I follow him to the shooting range. Commandos shoot from their hip, but he tells me to lie on the ground in order to use the automatic weapon.

"It might jump and you'd spray me."

I "chow down" almost daily with soldiers, unbeknownst to Mother. I am always home with her for meager meals. During this early stage of the war, Mother and I subsist mainly on legumes—wild avocados and wild squash. In sparse soil we raise pigeon peas, soybeans, and string beans, and we have a little trellis on which lima beans grow. Mother calls them "Lyman beans."

She shops at Oshima Grocery & Dry Goods Store. It's more fun to poke around here than at the Kaimukī supermarket where Grandpa shopped. Oshima's motto is, "If we don't have it, you don't need it." Mother found a black leather jacket; I told her *I needed it* to wear to school since it's sometimes chilly walking back and forth. (I wanted to cover my shameful scrawniness.)

Wartime means Oshima's is low on canned goods and fresh beef and has limited fresh fish—although some of the best fishing grounds in the world are off the Kona Coast. The army insists sampans—fishing boats—stay near shore. Everyone knows the *real fishing* is farther out.

Once in a while, Mother is given a chicken or a duck; it is my job to use a knife to kill and dress it. A soldier, describing himself as "A Catskill Mountains farm boy," teaches me how to "extinguish a chicken." He ties it overhead by its feet on the pipe next to our water storage tank and yanks its neck. Less messy than doing you know what with a hatchet.

I enjoy imaginary swordplay but hate real-life killing and eviscerating. But it's my job as "Man of the House" whenever Mother is given poultry.

New Yorkers, unlike Hawaiians, are unreserved and chatty. Soldiers get right to the point, talk fast, banter, and . . . well, *sound* different.

I'm beginning to know some Hawaiian men by now and observe how they talk among themselves in slow, easygoing, mellow conversation. Their laid-back voices rise from chests and stomachs, producing a "round sound." They speak softly ("unless you make them angry," I am told). Their words aren't always distinct and clear—you might have to listen carefully and maybe imagine the meaning. But whatever they say sounds melodic—unless they are *huhu,* meaning "provoked." The only time I heard a *huhu* Hawaiian was when Grandpa taught me about *insubordination!*

These New York soldiers have loud, constricted voices coming straight at you, piercing through their heads. "Upstaters" have flat-sounding a's and e's and use lots of "ey-ups," which mean "Yes." Those from "Nu Yahwk"— meaning the city—speak throaty "woids" (words). They use a guttural grunt when saying "Ye-ahh."

Mrs. Roberts, our principal's wife, teaches elocution so we'll vary our voice use. Classmates from Japanese-speaking homes use English shyly in a muffled monotone. She wants us to sound as if we're singing by changing tone and inflection.

For example, the sentence "As it is, I can't do it," is to be pronounced this way: *As eet ees* (using three tones on "is") . . . *I cah-n-t* (tones climb up four pitches on "cahn't") . . . *dew* . . . (tone slides down almost a octave on "dew") *eet!* (flat hard percussive sound on "eet").

Once past our initial embarrassment, it becomes fun to "sing" sentences. We chirp like mynah birds. (Mrs.

Roberts would be disappointed to know students speak that way only in her class.)

I ask Mrs. Roberts about haole soldiers' talk. At this point, I use the word "haole" as old-time Hawaiians did—to reference a "stranger" or "newcomer"—not as an inclusive label for Caucasians.

Mrs. Roberts explains: "They have regional dialects. New Yorkers' versions of local argot include county or borough patois and sounds. Brooklyn's vernacular is different than Buffalo's, for example." (I write many words she uses on vocabulary-building flash cards.)

We sound pretty similar in the Islands. Locals from everywhere—except for Caucasians—speak Pidgin. Not persons from Honolulu's private and English Standard Schools, though. "Proper English" is mandated there.

I inform the New Yorkers, using Mrs. Roberts' fancy speaking style. (Her elocution lessons involve high and low tones, pauses, and emphases.) Here is how I explain things to the soldiers:

"Pee-jen ees ah pawl-ee-gaht ov emm-ee-grahnt Eeng-lesh ahnd Hah-wah-ee-en wohds end phaw-ray-zezz."

Translation: "Pidgin is a polyglot of immigrant, English, and Hawaiian words and phrases." I overly exaggerate it for effect and then finish up with "local talk":

"I do da kine mo' good—Ri-igh-on da kini popo!"

I circle my thumb and forefinger and extend my fingers—creating an "OK" symbol.

They like it. From then on, when spotting me, some delightedly shout "Ri-igh-on" and raise the "OK" sign.

They sound almost, but n-o-t quite, local.

That's because it is almost impossible to change a lifetime of putting your tongue in a particular place. George Bernard Shaw covered this conundrum in *Pygmalion*. Mrs. Roberts suggested reading that book; Sumiko and I probably were the only ones who did.

I put menehunes and *perspectives* on hold. After-school and weekend life now involves New York soldiers. I'll retrospect and explain them.

The 27th Division, stationed around us, dates back to the Revolutionary War. It includes the "Fighting Irish"— the 69th Infantry Regiment—famous during the First World War.

I realize that these new neighbors are brave and capable soldiers because I saw *The Fighting 69th* movie at the new Waikīkī Theatre. James Cagney and fellow doughboys in that World War I movie spoke Brooklynese.

Before this war, Uncle Sam took me for a preshow organ concert featuring Edwin Sawtelle, the most famous organist in America, on the Hammond organ he'd helped to design. The Waikīkī Theatre was decorated as a tropical garden. Overhead, clouds, produced from dry ice, floated under the blue-sky ceiling while Maestro Sawtelle performed. It was expensive to hear an organ concert and see a first-run movie there—about $1.00 for an adult. I don't know what I cost.

This was Honolulu's grandest public luxury—apart from the fancy Royal Hawaiian, Moana, and Halekūlani Hotels, where movie stars and wealthy tourists lived for a month or so at a time. Those places weren't public though—locals weren't allowed on beaches in front of the hotels, because the sand belonged to the hotels. Waikīkī now belongs to the military. They put barbed wire along the shoreline to slow Japanese invaders

Soldiers come and go; the Fighting 69th transfers to Maui. That means I am no longer shooting a submachine gun—my pal took it with him. I've become close to "Captain Aloha," historian for the 27th Division, who travels a lot.

Kahu understands that I am living in the present among these new friends. I receive vicarious enjoyment from the stories soldiers tell me—I don't actually *experience* things as with menehune.

Mother and "Red," who is her military police boyfriend, are spending a lot of time together. They go to restaurants, take drives, and stuff for which a kid would be in the way. I continue to spend lots of time with books.

Now that I've put my personal story into *perspective* within this journal, I'm ready for the creative world that life brought me to and am eager to tell Per'fesser that *I'm done!*

A poster with photographs of burning and sinking Japanese aircraft carriers is displayed at the Kealakekua post office. America just had a major victory near Midway Island, 1,500 miles away! America's lost aircraft carriers appeared, and its pilots "crippled" Japan's marauding navy: "A Turning Point," the poster reports. GIs on Hospital Hill are grinning over our first World War II victory. Don't know much more; censorship controls what we learn.

It is June. I'd be thinking of summer vacation if attending school in Honolulu instead of in Kona. Vacation doesn't begin here until August, when coffee beans are red and ripe—classmates call them "cherries." School is scheduled so children can join parents in hand-picking the crop. Coffee mills pay farmers about $1.50 for a hundred-pound bag of beans, inspecting them for a ripe-red cherry look. Mother says families lease between three to five acres from the Bishop Estate, and income from coffee farmers' crops averages about $650 yearly. Mom and pop grocery stores advance credit against the harvest. Kids go home promptly to work after school since soil must be hoed loose and weeds pulled. Families raise chickens for eggs and have vegetable gardens.

Uncle Clarence Kumukoa Lyman attended the University of Hawai'i School of Agriculture with Uncle Bob, Mother's brother. He now works for the Department of Agriculture in Kona and raises rabbits to give to farmers. Uncle Clarence encourages farmers to pick abundant wild *honohono* grass: It's nourishing, free, and gives bunnies energy to multiply like . . . well, rabbits. "Rabbits are a good source of nourishing protein," he explained and demonstrated turning a wiggly rabbit into rabbit stew makings—supplementing my poultry knowledge.

"No, I don't want to build a cage and become a rabbit rancher," I hurriedly told him.

Whoops, my thoughts are traveling. Kahu is at the base of the eucalyptus tree and holding a mango. He's wearing a tan *malo*—a wrap-around loincloth—having worn out my shorts.

25. Ancient Hawaiian Life

Kahu pulls an elaborate-looking pair of glasses from under his *malo.* "Wear these for x-ray vision while we glide over Maui."

"To see like Superman?"

"Somewhat. They impose an image called 'augmented reality.' You will be able to identify *ahupua'a* boundaries as if Per'fesser outlined them for projection.

"We'll be in the mid-nineteenth century. Eat the mango. I want you to listen and read minds when we look in on a family."

"Will Miki join us?"

"No. While you prepared your perspective, Miki began composing a *Celtic Fairy Opera.* He says it has twenty-six varieties of fairies, from apparitions to witches, and includes 'The Choir of Giants,' known as 'The Stones of Stonehenge.' It's grand opera, more dramatic than Gilbert and Sullivan's *Iolanthe,* a fairy operetta.

"He works on it in a little corner in the lava tube, demanding 'Absolute quiet!' from Ah Soong and Rising Sun. They're curious about Miki's doings because he sings all the parts while composing it. You wouldn't recognize it was Miki, because he uses a wide range of voices."

Since we won't be walking, Kahu leans his paddle against the tree and then says, "Let's go."

I toss the mango seed in the bushes as Kahu reaches for my back. Instantly, we're several hundred feet above an island shaped with the mythical god Māui's head and shoulders. X-ray vision works: Sections of the land are colored with strips of red, orange, yellow, blue, indigo, and violet.

Soaring by my side, Kahu explains: "Colors denote the boundaries of land subdivisions. Those 100 to 100,000 outlined acres, called *ahupuaʻa*, reach from the mountains to the sea. *Ahupuaʻa* fed nearly a million residents before big white people discovered Hawaiʻi. Frequent wars kept population from expanding beyond Hawaiians' ability to raise enough food.

Each *ahupuaʻa* is a complete economic production system: forests and running streams in the mountains; flat land where crops grow; shore areas from where people harvest fin and shellfish, gather seaweed, and collect salt. Property lines run to the outer edge of the sea reef. Residents have access to all resources.

"Noncontiguous sections of land, called *ʻili kūpono,* are also unified under a single chief.

"Common people use *kōʻele,* small parcels, for their own use. The land system is designed to benefit the man on top; everyone works for him, as you'll find out."

He takes me over a series of freshwater and saltwater ponds. We swoop near those having passageways to the ocean and a series of connecting gates leading to the large inland pond.

Kahu explains: "To attract ocean fish, Hawaiians close off the large inner pond and open the gates leading to it while a lookout spots schools of fish. He signals for men to drop feed in the passages to lure fish. Once they're in, men close the gates and use feed trails to lure fish into the large pond. They become part of a food bank once in there.

"Before the white man came, Hawai'i's over 360 saltwater and freshwater fishponds produced 2 million pounds of fish a year.

"Hawai'i is the only place in the Pacific with the type of *aquaculture* you see here. Menehune deserve the credit: We carved gulches, built waterways, and established ponds. We also planted sweet potatoes and pumpkins where there wasn't room to grow. Hawaiians continued these practices.

Kahu directs me to *'ili kūpono:* "Water is directed into these taro ponds from streams. *Kanaka* raise fish in them; fish droppings are nutrients that help taro grow.

"When Tahitians became Hawaiians, they continued what menehune initiated. Before they came here, we left trails behind of our accomplishments: vegetable pounders, peelers, and other stone tools.

"Per'fesser says, 'Archeologists will discover them in Indonesia and elsewhere some day.' He claims 'It will help the world to realize how accomplished little people were while mankind was still in a rudimentary stage'"

We land on a ledge overlooking a valley. Large numbers of people work in the taro ponds stretching over several acres. I watch them bent over and weeding, just as I did on Grandpa's dry land.

Kahu continues his orientation: "Hawaiians lived under very distinctive pecking orders. Kings, chiefs, and landlords were *ali'i,* the royal class. Areas of land, sometimes an island, were under the control of the *ali'i 'ai moku*—the district ruler.

"The *ali'i 'ai moku* distributed the *ahupua'a* and *'ili kūpono* under his control to his loyal chiefs to manage. Lesser chiefs, known as *konohiki,* were landlords who parceled out portions of the *ahupua'a* to the *maka'āinana*— commoners and tenants of the land. Those are the kinds of people you are seeing working. The *konohiki* oversaw the use and distribution of water throughout lands in their charge and designated certain fish to be reserved for the landlord or for the king."

We glide near a taro patch where a family is working. The middle-aged man is on his knees, apparently unable to bend over. Two youths are adjacent; the taller one weeds vigorously while the other, slighter in size, weeds gracefully as though following a rhythm.

I sense we'll visit them. Kahu continues explaining: "Hawaiians were classed into three types: *ali'i* or chiefs and *maka'āinana* or commoners. I will explain the other class, a form of "untouchables" known as *kauwā,* or slaves, when we visit *heiau.*"

Maka'āinana grew crops, caught fish, raised pigs, cut trees, and built canoes. They provided tribute to landlords.

I am surprised to see Per'fesser sitting on a stone property line marker. Kahu explains what it is. When we're close enough, Per'fesser starts chattering away.

"Aloha. I came to make sunrise sketches in Haleakalā, the House of the Sun, for a canvas I'm about to start. Haleakalā is the only place in the world with silversword plants—stalks are over six feet high, it has silvery gray leaves and maroon flowers. It's too cold up there for Aiko, so I'll sketch a cluster of plants and blooms for reference, return to warm Kaua'i, and paint a large canvas of her surrounded by silverswords at sunrise."

Per'fesser seems giddy and garrulous in describing his latest Aiko adventure. I nod agreeably.

His mannerism changes suddenly, and he begins a serious lecture.

"You are seeing Hawai'i today while at the peak of its feudal system. Ambitious Hawaiian kings and chiefs built realms for themselves—analogous to what kings and lords did in England, where they subordinated the common people, established an oppressive feudal system, and called their serfs to arms to fight bloody wars."

He continues rather vehemently, proclaiming what my Uncle Sam would describe as "A liberal's perspective."

"Here in Hawai'i, all property—everything from one's own children to the home site, the canoe, and the stone axe—belongs to the king. The people own nothing. They are kept in their place by a complicated system of *kapu* proclaimed by king, chief, or priest.

"The king is over all the people. The yearly harvest is his; at his whim he can dispossess chiefs as well as commoners.

"After a battle in which a king acquires additional territory, he distributes lands among his loyal generals."

Kahu interrupts: "Per'fesser presents a stern picture. He has spent so much time as a liberal academic—not living the ancient Hawaiian life.

"'*Kapu*,' meaning 'forbidden,' is the regulation system in effect down there. On Kaua'i you heard Kekuni think about not stepping on Kuali'i's shadow. Breaking a *kapu*—even unintentionally—meant immediate death.

"It is *kapu* to look directly at a chief, intrude on his space, or be in sight of him with your head higher than his.

"Places that are *kapu* may be marked by two crossed staffs, each with a white ball atop. They're seen in coves where fish spawn, sometimes in places noted for a chief's favorite fish.

"The *kapu* system governs contact between men and women. Here, *kapu* guides Hawaiians' life or leads to their death.

"Let's gain a perspective from that family over there. They're *pau hana*—finished with work for the day. Makua is the father, Mama is the mother, Mona is the daughter, the smaller brother is Loka, and I'ini is the large guy.

"Per'fesser, would you like to join us?"

He shakes his head, "No, I need to go to Haleakalā to sketch. Arthur, have you organized your perspectives since I've seen you last?"

"Yes, all is recorded in my journal."

This seems to please him, and he walks away.

Kahu and I follow the father and two sons returning to the family's living complex—a group of stick houses covered with grass. Kahu explains, "Those are called *kauhale:* Each dwelling has its own purpose, a typical Hawaiian living complex."

He points to and explains what I see: "This is a typical family living area. That shack is where women eat; the little covered area nearby is where the husband prepares her food. Women are forbidden to eat pork, breadfruit, coconuts, bananas, certain fowl, shark meat, and some other good things.

"The *mua,* that thatched shack on the other side, is where men eat; the covered cooking shack near it is where men prepare their own food. Everyone sleeps in the *hale noa* in the center—food is not allowed in there. The thatched house at the far right is where a woman is isolated each month and when she is pregnant. During other monthly *kapu* periods, women cannot ride in canoes or be close with men.

"Those large shacks to the left are where crops are stored. Beyond is where Mama keeps her *lauhala* weaving supplies. This is old-style living, with a separate shack for each function and to perpetuate *kapu.*"

We follow I'ini and his father into the *hale noa.* Spears are placed against the far wall, opposite the entrance.

I'ini asks, "When I get married, where might I live and raise my own family? This land is allocated to you."

Makua answers, "You might be able to move in here unless our chief decides I won't be good enough in battle . . . or if he loses this *ahupua'a* in another one of the wars he loves . . . or if he thinks the spear thrust in my thigh weakened my leg so I won't be able to shove in a melee. And if that's the case, he might offer me on the altar. Then the *konohiki* will assign this land to someone else, and you'll be out. Or maybe he'll let you make your own deal with him. Then you'll become part of his quota system.

"But of course, you'll have to take care of Mama.

"I noticed how impatiently you were while working today. Is it because at sixteen you are thinking of marriage and wanting to be on your own?"

I'ini moves his head indefinitely and sort of twitches.

His father continues: "Just remember: An ordinary Hawaiian husband is never on his own. A man has to acquire food and prepare separate meals for himself and his wife. He and his wife eat separately in specific houses he makes for that purpose. Pretty soon, he has to build a cluster of houses like these here. He has to make time to practice with weapons, because farmers become warriors at the call of an *ali'i*.

"If you think life is confining working in a taro pond, consider husbandly—and eventually fatherly—responsibilities ahead. It is far less complicated to live with a man. That's what your brother Loka has in mind.

"By the way, Oh'i, the pig raiser, is interested in Mona. He offered his heaviest breeding sow for her."

I'ini appears shocked. "Why would you give her to that old man? He's worn out three wives! He'd send her all over the *ahupua'a* gathering breadfruit for his pigs. A *kahuna* killed Oh'i's last wife because she picked bananas for the pigs. The *kahuna* said it's *kapu* for women even to touch bananas!"

"What if he threw in some suckling pigs with the sow?"

"No!" retorts I'ini. "Mona is too pretty, too smart, and too kind to be replaced by pigs. Let's wait until

199

Makahiki. She can't rise above her class, but someone more promising than Oh'i may catch her eye. I won't marry unless a woman understands I take care of Mona. She'll be a good *kupuna*."

Kahu taps me on the shoulder and says, "Let's fly away. These are family matters; we'll see them again at the Makahiki."

Back in Kona under the eucalyptus tree, Kahu gestures for me to sit down, and he explains the system with a more kindly slant than Per'fesser's.

"*Kapu* were ancient Hawaiian laws. The Royal Kolowalu Statute was the best law, and it was created during the reign of Kuali'i Kuniakea Kunikealaikauaokalani. That is King Kuali'i's full name.

"His statute was for the care and preservation of life; it was for aged men and women to lie down in the road with safety; it was to encourage husbandmen and fishermen to be kind to strangers, to help the hungry.

"Kuali'i's law stated that if a man says, 'I am hungry,' feed him. For he is claiming his rights by swearing the Kolowalu law by his mouth, whereby food becomes free. The owner cannot withhold. Food from those who are better off is free to the less fortunate.

"Anyone under King Kuali'i's command must observe the law or be punished. Under application of this law, a transgressor, or someone who is about to die for taking food, is exonerated of death or any other penalty. This was a major change under the old order. Mercy had been unknown. Kuali'i's merciful law forgave the hungry.

"However, if someone is simply *robbing* another's food or property, this law does not apply. Severe punishment is dealt to the thief."

I reiterate what I understand. "Kuali'i's law meant that a hungry person asking for help should receive charity. A person taking food that he needs is forgiven. Those who rob because they are greedy are punished."

"Yes," Kahu says, then disappears.

The Battle of Midway had energized GIs on Hospital Hill. When the Fighting 69th was transferred to Maui, Captain Aloha went there and told me, "They're practicing ship-to-shore landing on the beaches."

I knew what that meant. Soldiers took me down to a bay in Kona ("Keep it secret!" I was told). I watched them operate an LCI designed to transport troops in shallow water.

I was with Mother as she drove past Kohala lava fields where marines practiced shooting howitzers. Large, empty brass shell casings were by the road. She wouldn't stop the car for me to pick up souvenirs. "I'm a government employee and can't allow you to do that," she said. Smart mouth me replied, "Yeah, but we're only a territory and that's not really like being part of the United States government." She kept driving and muttered, "We're under martial law—everything is government controlled."

True, it's why fisherman no longer can catch *aku* (tuna). The government thinks local men on sampans might tell secrets to Japanese on submarines that might be cruising in Hawaiian waters. "Selling secrets" might be more lucrative than fishing.

Cooks at the mess complain about "gremlins" getting into their refrigerators—seems they steal ice cubes, leaving empty trays on the table. "Do you know anything about this, Arthur? Are you a gremlin?"

I shake my head and say the only Italian word I know—except for lasagna: "*No Capisce!* I wouldn't do mischief that would make chow downs *kapu.*" (I think they thought I finished my protest with a sneeze—*Achoo!*)

Captain Aloha said Gremlins originated in England, where they fool around with the Royal Air Force's airplanes and cause what are called "snafus."

I realize Queen Esther has sent menehune to pilfer ice so she can enjoy *cold* fruit drinks. I won't say anything, but there are *no gremlins* in Kona.

The Rev. Miller has turned the church's recreational building into a military USO—a place for GIs to read, relax, and play table games. I've attended evening socials; civilian food is scarce, but good folk of Christ Church Episcopal share what they are able. Servicemen especially enjoy cake, homemade peanut butter cookies, fresh milk from a local dairy—and *wow—Kona coffee!*

These guys like to sing. Captain Aloha gave me a printed copy of what they sang while ships transported them to Hawai'i. Lots are World War I songs; not many have been written about this war yet—except the one everyone sings vigorously: "Let's remember Pearl Harbor."

One GI from Syracuse has a fine tenor voice and is always asked to perform "The Prisoner's Song." It's what a convict expresses, he sings of his sweetheart the night before he is to die.

He says "Sparky," America's first electric chair, is in Auburn near his home city. Electricity was transmitted from Niagara Falls to "Sparky"—and elsewhere in New York state, of course, is what he means. He sings the plaintive melody so well, giving everyone a catch in their throat. Maybe GIs are thinking of what they possibly face as America tries to win back what Japan has taken.

Rev. Miller puts a croquet field on the grass behind the parsonage, and I try to practice whacking balls through the hoops because I am good at marbles; croquet has some similar tactics. "Red," the MP who is mother's friend, puts his big-booted foot on his ball next to mine that he's just hit, then blasts mine out of play—really far, almost into the bushes. I can't do the same to his ball because, what if I used all of my pent-up energy trying to do the same thing and smashed my bare foot with the mallet?

I was improving my skills one morning during the 8:00 a.m. Communion service—I attend the one at 10:00 a.m. During our next Tuesday review, the Rev. Miller asked me not to play croquet until I heard the final hymn. "It sounds like the Devil's knocking on the church door," is what he said.

Rev. Miller is creating something interesting in his workshop. On his lathe, he's turning out wooden chessmen almost three feet high. He plans to introduce communal chess at the USO. "It'll encourage GIs to discuss strategies and help them to really appreciate the game," he explained. He's a thoughtful man who tries to help people understand things.

26. Feudalism

We are sitting under the eucalyptus tree, now my clubhouse. Kahu is talking about "Hawai'i's Classical Age," the time period into which we've traveled. "Protocol," seemingly, relates to everything in it. That word means "proper procedure," he explains.

After several of James Fenimore Cooper's books, I know about surprise attacks and how Indians sought individual glory by counting coups and taking scalps. I ask Kahu, "Do Hawaiian warriors ambush the enemy?"

His response is surprising: "A Hawaiian warrior who kills an unprepared enemy is considered a criminal. He is clubbed to death or eviscerated on a temple's altar.

"Warfare is never conducted without preliminary rituals. Typically, those involve prayer and human sacrifice on a *heiau* stone. A priest seeks omens about the battle to interpret."

Attention isn't centered on him: The sulking actor wants to be heard.

Kahu nods to Miki, whimpering like a puppy. Kahu explains to me, "He wants to describe Hawaiian rituals."

Miki's face brightens as he struts forward, then stands—legs spread, elbows bent, hands on his hips—his lecturing stance—to explain:

> Ancient warfare's rules and formalities
> Involved gods and many ceremonies:
> Build a *heiau* for human sacrifice—
> Intimidation is part of the price.
> Put a feather on top of a god's head,
> (The local Delphic Oracle instead),
> Chopped down coconut tree declares a 'war,'
> A stone answers: White, *talk;* Black, *war's not far.*

Although smiling, my mind wanders away from Miki. I think about how Kahu uses several different speaking styles: brief when we interact—he delivers succinct information, that's it; explanations are extensive detailed stories; personal conversational style is cordial but to the point. He doesn't waste words and says little about himself, doesn't express personal feelings. Experience with Grandpa, and now with Kahu, makes me realize that depersonalizing yourself is a male Hawaiian characteristic: carried-over traditional stoicism?

My ukulele teacher Mr. Hua behaves similarly. He is friendly, kind, extremely patient, and reassuring. Only within his family's social environment do I learn how he *feels.* Hawaiians call this *ha'aha'a*—being unpretentious.

I find out about his good qualities from others.

When interacting, Mr. Hua, grandfather, and Kahu share the Hawaiian characteristic of being direct and objective. They speak quietly, self-effacingly.

By contrast, Kahu's stories, explanations, and historical descriptions are detailed and colorful. I now realize why: Those are compilations of stories *handed down to him.* He is a repository of information, containing wisdom told by many voices and compiled over long periods of time. He reflects varied experiences. He is not expressing personal dogma.

I will now listen carefully as Kahu amplifies Miki's brief verse.

"As a prelude to the war he is planning, a *mōʻī* might order a *luakini heiau* built on massive stone platforms on his home island. This requires thousands of laborers. Menehune, wonderful stoneworkers, have built many *heiau*. But we avoid projects meant to start wars. Menehune build agricultural *heiau,* to venerate life.

"The *heiau* of a war-planning *mōʻī* cannot be kept a secret. Word reaches the foe. The *mōʻī* uses *heiau* construction to intimidate his enemy. Everyone knows there will be human sacrifices and elaborate ceremonies to seek a god's approval for the war.

"Such a *heiau* includes a god made from branches of wood covered in *kapa* bark cloth. A feather suspended from the top of the god's head moves in the breeze. The priest interprets the movement as either favorable or unfavorable for war."

Winking Miki wants me to realize Hawaiians weren't the first to practice psychological warfare. He says:

> A virgin was the soothsayer B.C.,
> Delphic Oracle who battles foresees.
> Drugged and speaking gibberish to a priest,
> He'd explain the outcome and who would feast.

I reflect that watching a spaced-out, beautiful Pythia—the predicting priestess—"speak in tongues" would be more intriguing than waiting for a feather to waft in the breeze. Socrates, Plato, and Aristotle referred to Pythia and the Oracles. I know this—where else but from *The Book of Knowledge!*

Miki's experience over so many centuries adds geographic perspective, dimension, and correlation to Kahu's teachings. I am beginning to feel comfortable about believing Miki; he's laughing at himself, not mocking me.

Kahu elaborates on one of Miki's lines: "The cutting down of a coconut tree within an opponent's territory was a brazen and usually irrevocable declaration of war. Ancients compared a tree to a man. The head of the coconut was under the earth, and its fruit—the testicles—swung above. If the tree was cut down, the man would wilt."

Kahu continues: "Responding with a white stone indicates a willingness to discuss differences. Delivering a black stone means war is imminent.

"After exchanging stones, respective sides gather for a council of war. Adversaries discuss differences—responding to the white stone. Or they determine battle guidelines—responding to the black stone. The reason leading to the conflict is debated and settled. It is all quite formalized. The battle I took you to see exemplified that formality."

I nod: "And we saw that debate's outcome."

"Correct. Prebattle formalities set the stage for Pelei'oholani allowing Alapa'i's army to live and leave. Such old-time ways will disappear.

"Let's go to Puna." He touches my back.

There we see stone walls, built of large slabs, surrounding open areas. We stroll within the walls. Kahu explains: "This is Waha'ula. It is Hawai'i's first *luakini heia,u* the kind used for human sacrifices. The voyager priest Pāʻao from Tahiti built it to honor the war god Kūkāʻilimoku, whom he introduced to Hawaiʻi. Prior to Pāʻao's arrival, sometime before 1200 B.C., the only *heiau* were those built by menehune, honoring life.

"Pāʻao initiated the social order that separates *aliʻi,* kahuna, *makaʻāinana,* and the *kauwā* class of outcasts. Menehune considered each other equal. We chose our leader, even that one who ordered our Kauaʻi exodus."

This *heiau* is constructed of lava rock walls built into a rectangular formation. From what I've read of *heiau,* I know it had raised terrace platforms for shacks or other structures. Wooden carved figures, representing gods, were placed in and around it.

Kahu explains more: "*Kapu* breakers and defeated warriors were brought here to be killed. Some reached a *puʻuhonua,* the place of refuge, before being captured. A priest there could absolve them. One such place was Puʻuhonua o Hōnaunau, also on this island."

"It's next to the ocean in Hōnaunau," I say. "It's where my blond Hawaiian friend Billy lives; we've swum and speared fish. I was near a large sting ray."

Kahu reaches to take me somewhere, grabbing my hand. Miki rides along.

We are at another *luakini heiau.* Miki whispers, eerily:

> Defeated soldiers, slaves marked with tattoos,
> And all the *kapu* violators too,
> Clubbed to death *there* on that square altar stone.
> Six-foot-high outside walls hid why they moaned:
> Knowing the horror that's awaiting them,
> Eviscerate, flay—both women and men.

Miki's accomplished his purpose: The sun is hot here in the Ka'ū lava-covered area; he's provided chills.

Kahu explains: "Large stones weren't near this *heiau*. Long lines of men had to pass them, hand-to-hand, from a quarry miles away.

"It was terribly hot working in the blazing sun. The priest and workers decided on revenge.

"An enormous ohia tree, symbol of a god, was being moved into the *heiau*. Workers pulling on the rope pretended they couldn't move the tree up the steep hill.

"The priest told the king, 'We'll never overcome that god's resistance if you walk in front of him. A *kapu* against his shadow falling on you—condemning anyone else to death—doesn't apply because that tree's a god and a shade tree to boot.'

"King Koha'okalani moved beneath the 'god' to help push him up the slope. The priest and people instantly released the rope. The enormous tree 'god' rolled down and crushed the king. The conniving priest ate the king's eyeballs, as other conspirators cheered.

"Those were savage times. Pulling out and eating the heart of an enemy on a battlefield was a kingly thing to do by followers of Kūkāi'ilimoku."

Miki's whispered horror story was mild compared to Kahu's. I have more shivers; the sun doesn't feel hot at all.

"Let's return," Kahu says, walking toward me. "Even without huge replicas of gods and ceremonial buildings on it, the stone platform of this *heiau* is a stark reminder of the horrors Pā'ao of Tahiti introduced. The aura remains as a curse."

27. Taxes and Games

This is October: Dusk comes earlier, skies stay dark longer, rains fall harder, seas are rougher. We're on the coffee-picking school vacation break. I'm eager to see Kahu, sitting under the tree; he begins talking as I walk up.

"Lono, god of agriculture and fertility, brings this weather to nurture soil, letting it rest.

Kahu has begun one of his compressed lectures. I listen intently. He never quizzes me, just layers one set of facts on another, expecting me to catch the gist.

"Rituals make it appear that common people are repaying Lono for his yearlong gifts. *Maka'āinana* actually are paying taxes to chiefs for the privilege of living and working.

"Most *kapu* are suspended, although women still can't eat with men, and many foods remain forbidden to them. Wars are postponed. Services at royal *heiau* are suspended—no ritual killings. Makahiki is the best time to be Hawaiian.

"Commoners prepare and store food in advance: They salt and dry fish, pound taro into hard poi, which they'll save, and add water to it before eating. Farmers bake and dry sweet potatoes and breadfruit.

"Stand up. We're off to Maui to look in on the family we visited earlier. I brought a mango for you. While you eat, I'll explain what we'll see."

It's a Haden; guess I'll be reading thoughts. Kahu continues my orientation.

"Commoners prepare gifts for Lono during eight months of the year: Women beat *kapa*—turning bark into cloth for royal men and women's garments. They plait baskets and weave mats from *hala* leaves. Men grow taro, sweet potatoes, yams, bananas, coconuts, breadfruit, and other crops. They raise pigs, dogs, and chickens for food variety. Oceanside dwellers salt and dry fish and squid. Woodcrafters carve wooden bowls and platters. Birders collect yellow, black, and red feathers to make royal capes, helmets, *kāhili,* and leis.

"Whatever one can grow, catch, or make is offered to Lono through his royal emissary, the area's chief.

"As I explained during our last trip to Maui, *maka'āinana,* working people, don't own the land upon which they live. Theoretically, it belongs to the gods and is managed by the chiefs. Under chiefly guidance, people are allowed to use resources of the land. For that right, they offer goods they produce to the chiefs—who accept it on behalf of the gods.

"You've about finished your mango; toss it away and we'll watch as the Maui farming family observes Makahiki."

"No Miki?"

"No Miki. He's added Queen Esther's dryad friends to his opera, claiming they're more appealing than the Druid Queen and courtiers Bellini concocted for *Norma*—whatever that means. I don't know the difference between Druid and dryad; the only opera I know is the *Menehune Opera*."

But I know! Uncle Buster Cook says Rosa Ponselle has the most beautiful voice of the century. We listened to NBC broadcast her aria from *Norma,* Bellini's opera about Druids who fought the Romans. He promises he'll teach more about opera as time goes on. I do know that Hans Christian Andersen wrote about a *dryad* who traveled to Paris in an oak tree. Reading adds dimension to my life.

I toss the mango seed into the bushes. Kahu starts explaining.

"Makahiki begins with an around-the-island tax trip, with Lono making his ritual visit. That's what we'll see first. To show gratitude for the year gone by, Hawaiians offer Lono gifts that chiefs willingly accept for him. Then everyone enjoys sports, games, and pursuit of pleasure."

I feel his touch just before Kahu and I land near a pile of stones. On the top of the pile is a carved wooden pig's head.

"This is the boundary of the *ahupua'a* we visited earlier," Kahu explains. "The *ahu* over there is where gifts to Lono are presented. People in this *ahupua'a* have cleaned it up and rebuilt that altar. Makahiki starts for them here; the hundred or so residents have piles of gifts for Lono."

The two boys I'd seen earlier are carrying an older woman in a woven sling. It's similar to the one holding old King Kuali'i at the poetic battle. The boys' father and sister stand by piles of food and heaps of mats. The boys gently place the sling on the ground—that's Mama in it, probably. They help their father pile the family's gifts on the altar. Their sister stands off to the side with the old woman, whom I notice has only one leg.

"This is your opportunity to observe an old-time family's social relations," Kahu explains. "I want you to experience their dynamics. When a teenager, Mama lost her right leg to a shark while diving for *wana*—the sea urchins Hawaiians love so much. An outstanding swimmer with amazing breath control, she went outside the bay into deep sea caves. She had scraped *wana* off the cave walls and was bringing them up to Papa and his pals in a canoe when the shark struck. They banged the shark with their paddles and pulled her into the canoe. She was beautiful and known for her mana—supernatural power. While she was helpless and in pain, Papa ardently declared that he wanted to marry her."

Kahu excitedly says, "Here comes Lono!"

A strange sort of parade heads toward us, led by something overhead; it's too large to be a kite.

The procession approaches the altar. On top of an approximately twelve-foot pole is the carved replica of a head—it must be Lono's. A crosspiece is attached to Lono's neck and long white pieces of *kapa* hang from it. Feather leis are tied at the ends of the crosspiece. Draped at each side of the crosspiece are albatross, huge birds that fly over the sea. These look as if they came from a taxidermist's shop; glittering green stones used for eyes must be olivine; Mother says they're also called peridot. Pele creates them.

The priestly process walks toward the altar—ocean to their left, mountains to their right, *kapa* spreading in the wind like a sail.

Kahu explains: "Priests make their round-the-island tour in a clockwise direction. People realize the image at the top of the pole, being carried throughout the district, is Lono's spirit. A *kahuna* prayed it would be transmitted to the twelve-foot-high pole they carry.

"Residents of each *ahupua'a* anticipate a visit from Lono's spirit prior to Makahiki. The *konohiki,* chief in charge of the *ahupua'a,* collects gifts for Lono. The common people believe he will present them to Lono. "

"Theirs is not to reason why," I hear from a sardonic voice behind me. "This is not an obvious and direct route into the king's treasury, as Queen Esther describes in her stories of Persia's yearly festival. Why do Hawaiian chiefs want war? For King Xerxes' reason: To expand the land from which they'll receive taxes—in the guises of 'gifts to Lono.' Don't expect that this god will receive any more Makahiki largesse than fits into a small canoe."

Per'fesser is back with us. An artist's large sketching pad sticks out of his knapsack. "Beautiful reds, oranges, vermilions, all shades of crimson burst into color on Haleakalā this morning," he exults. "I brought my brightest colored pencils in anticipation. They provide only a hint; recreating the full splendor will require inspired mixing of oil paint."

He comments again on the ceremony as *maka'āinana* prepare to present their offerings: "Accepting Lono's appearance in this procession is why Hawaiians will think Captain Cook is Lono when, a few years from now, he sails in on the HMS *Resolution,* with its high crosspieces and billowing sails."

"Let's not go into that, Per'fesser," Kahu admonishes. "We're here to see the Makahiki. Come along, if you wish."

"Bubbling Miki's not with you? Nah. Am eager to be back in Kaua'i to tell Aiko how radiant Haleakalā was this morning. Can't wait to turn my pencil sketches into oil. Take a look, Arthur."

He opens his sketchpad: Per'fesser has become an Impressionist! Vibrant colors and abstract images almost jump off each page—so different from the dark, evocative Pre-Raphaelite kinds of paintings in his cave. Per'fesser has equaled demigod Māui's achievement by *capturing the sun!*

"Ah hum!" Kahu calls my attention to this ceremony we came to see.

Priests stop at the altar. People carry gifts to Lono.

"The *kahuna* representing Lono is signaling with a nod of his head that gifts are acceptable," Kahu explains. "Woe, if he shakes his head. Persons failing to win approval are evicted by the end of Makahiki."

The *kahuna* just nods.

Kahu explains what happens next.

"After a brief ceremony, the *kahuna* declares all land is free from *kapu.* He will hold Lono's image face down as the group leaves for the next *ahupua'a,* his eyes fixed approvingly at land from where gifts came.

"Lono will be looking up and forward when approaching the next *ahupua'a.* Warriors standing in the back over there are packing the tribute for the *ali'i nui,* the high chief, who rules for Lono. He'll share the bounty with district chiefs."

"It's really booty," Per'fesser interrupts sarcastically.

Pretending he didn't hear, Kahu continues: "It is understood that chiefs rule the land for the gods and receive everything as Lono's representatives on earth."

I ask, "Once their year's labor is carried away, what comes next?"

"The second phase begins: celebration, feasting, and sporting events. Tonight at midnight everyone cleanses themselves in the sea or in a pond, figuratively ridding themselves of the past year's impurities. Then they'll dress in their best. No work will be done for four months.

"Let's enjoy the excitement."

The family of five is returning to their dwelling group. Mama has a peaceful expression on her face as sons I'ini and Loka carry her in the sling.

Her tribute—intricately woven *hala* mats, some almost room size—excited the priests. They seemed particularly impressed by artistic patterns she included in varying dyed shades. While one *kahuna* examines an intricate design, Per'fesser comments: "She's eidetic. Mama has incredible perception. Genius memory enables her to retain everything she sees. Those become elements she transforms into artistry."

Per'fesser wanders away, eager to show Aiko *his* new form of artistry, I guess.

I sense Kahu wants me to observe the Maui family's teenagers. Kahu has the ability to take me in and out of the time periods. That is how I will journalize about Makahiki. It lasts for four months, but through menehune magic, Kahu provides *flash forwards* like this one.

I'ini walks over to a spear-throwing contest. Kahu explains: "This is called *'ō'ō ihe*. Into stalks of banana plants, contestants will throw the kinds of spears Hawaiian warriors use to pierce the bodies of enemies. Sturdy wood stakes have been driven into the ground here. Banana stalks, cut into six-foot lengths, are tied to them. A six-foot man is considered an idealized warrior, so the banana stalk symbolizes an enemy."

This is what I witness: The referee calls *"Ho'omākaukau!"* (Get ready!). Each contestant steps up to the line, about fifteen feet from the stalks, grasps the middle of his spear, holds it high, points, and aims at the banana stalk. The referee shouts *"'Oia!"* (Start!). They hurl spears toward the juicy trunks of the banana trees. Then they retrieve their spears from the stalk and return to the throwing line.

Those whose spears missed or didn't stick in the stalk are out of the contest. I'ini's spear is so deeply embedded in the symbolic enemy that he has to twist to remove it.

This is a wonderful spectator sport: The crowd on hillsides can watch the flight of the spears as they pierce the targets and remain there or see them miss the mark and drop to the field beyond.

Competitors return to the throwing line, now moved three feet farther back. The referee again calls *"'Oia!"* Spears fly, then are retrieved. The same rules apply: If a spear misses or fails to stick, the disappointed thrower leaves the field. Starting point for the next try is an additional three feet away. The contest continues until I'ini, the only remaining competitor, stands seventy feet from his mutilated target. He is hailed as "The Champion!"

I'ini walks to another part of the field that's marked off with stakes and cords. Kahu says, "He'll compete in *ihe pahe'e,* a spear-sliding contest. This demonstrates throwing strength and accuracy."

Five-foot spears with blunt heads are stacked there. Two players face each other at opposite ends of the field. The referee calls *"Ho'omākaukau!"* Grasping his spear a little forward of its middle, I'ini points the heavy blunt end toward the stakes. At the call of *"'Oia!"* I'ini bends low and with an underhand thrust slides the spear along the surface of the field with sufficient force to send it between the stakes onto his partner, who plays catcher for I'ini, the pitcher.

"Each slide between the stakes is a point for him," Kahu explains. "He'll keep stepping back, making each succesive slide longer."

His partner slides the spear back along the grass and, on command, I'ini slides the blunt spear through the stakes. Soon, I'ini's partner, having less arm strength, is walking forward before attempting to slide the spear to I'ini.

I'ini has the highest total score for spear sliding. The crowd cheers, and several men cluster around him conversing excitedly.

"What's going on?" I ask.

"An ardent group that practices battle skills has invited him to train with their militia; they practice near where his family farms.

"Listen to what I'ini is thinking."

These men said our king bestows mana—privilege and power—on esteemed warriors. I could win his attention by performing well in battle. The way of the koa is for me. I'll start training with them when Makahiki ends.

"He's made his decision," Kahu tells me. "Observe."

I'ini walks to his new friends and says, "I'll be joining you." They exchange warrior *honi*. I'ini finds his parents and tells them, "I'm filled with energy. I have the chance to train and elevate myself from stoop labor. I'll become so respected that no chief will push you off the farm."

Kahu puts his hand on my shoulder to guide me away. "Now that you know about I'ini, let's look in on Loka."

With another flash forward, we sit on a hill along with a crowd of people looking down on a hula performance.

We're too far away to hear what kinds of sounds the precision group below follows in their dance.

"What's happening, Kahu?"

"Male dancers are doing hula *kahiko,* with intricate steps and hand motions illustrating a chanter's words. This dance tells about Ka'ulahea I, *mō'ī* of Maui, father of great kings of the Hawaiian Islands. He is the great progenitor of Kekaulike, your ancestor Pelei'oholani, Kalaniopu'u, Kahekili, Kamehameha, and many other chiefs of Hawai'i. The famous Kuali'i married his daughter Kalanikahimakeiali'i and was his son-in-law.

"No war occurred between Maui and any other island during his reign. Just being able to hear his name spoken and to rise and cheer, now that there is no *kapu,* is a big treat for the crowd."

The crowd has quieted down; now we hear the name of the *mō'ī* called out behind us. I look up from where we sit. Loka is chanting and dancing on the hill. Although we can't see detailed steps of dancers down below, seemingly he is duplicating them.

"Is he permitted to do this, Kahu?"

"No *kapu* during Makahiki," he answers.

Loka has a fern lei on his head; his long black hair gleams from oil. He wears a loose brownish *kapa* garment; Mama's intricate decorations are printed on it. Loka moves his lips to words of the chant, his hands flutter, feet motions are rhythmical, his animated face expresses varying emotions—mostly joy.

The family is here: Mama leans against Mona, mouthing the words—she is cueing Loka. Makua and I'ini watch proudly.

"You are viewing Mama's miraculous powers," Kahu explains. "Loka dances and voices the words, but crippled Mama makes it possible. Per'fesser used a strange word to describe her gift."

"'Eidetic memory' is what he said."

"Although she may see something for only brief seconds, she recalls it vividly in perfect detail. She has observed great hula dancers, analyzed their moves, and knows the chants. She's taught this to her son. Watch— she mouths the words before Loka performs a movement. She puts directions into his head, making him carefree, able to concentrate all of his energy into the dance, to react spontaneously, without having to rely on memory!

"Hula *kahiko* requires very strict discipline; a dancer can be punished severely for making a mistake—especially when doing ritualistic *heiau* dances. Having Mama as his coach, possessing some of her memory gifts himself, makes Loka a phenomenal dancer!

"Look over there! His future is approaching."

Word of what Loka is doing has reached officials below. Some have come up to watch. Important-looking people are talking with the family. Trouble? No! Everyone is grinning. Loka is twisting around in an improvised dance of joy! He's gyrating his hips so fast—he's dancing Tahitian.

Kahu says, "The head of Maui's most prestigious *halau* has invited this boy genius to move in after Makahiki."

"That leaves only Mona without future plans."

"She's gifted, too," Kahu answers. "Let's move forward in time and watch her."

There won't be outdoor recreation today. Sheets of rain pour down on the large *hale* built for this purpose. It is the recreational center for children while vacationing adults enjoy daytime sleep. Mona is here with the kids and everyone's busy. She seems peripatetic—continually moving throughout the *hale,* keeping everyone busy. About fifty children from five to about twelve years old are here. She shows a group of eight-year-old youngsters how to use fingers on both hands to make string figures. They catch on quickly and contest each other for the fastest, weirdest, most artful shape. Some ask, "Guess what this is?" She brought checkerboards and bags containing black stones and white coral. She instructs an older boy in the rudiments, and he shows others. She moves to another age group and presents a quick course in riddling called *ʻōlelo nane.*

Kids ask, "Is it story time, Mona?"

"Soon," she replies. "But first, I want this group to change places with that group and try another game." More story-time requests lead to moving kids along for even another game.

Then, in a loud voice, she addresses the group: "Let me teach you something new, then I'll describe a list of stories. You can vote on which story to hear first."

She calls out: "Moki!"

A boy about my age raises his hand. He's the checker champ. I've watched players come to the corner where he squats before a board. He responds to their tentative moves with a few rapid ones of his own; they walk away dumfounded, shaking their heads.

Mona addresses Moki, but she is really speaking to the entire group because everyone is listening: "You and I have practiced some proverbs and they are good lessons for life. Proverbs will be a new experience for this group, so I want you to help me demonstrate the procedure. I'll tell a story. You'll explain its meaning. Is that fine with you?"

Moki grins, nodding his head enthusiastically. I think we have an actor in the *hale*.

"She's a really good teacher," I whisper to Kahu.

Don't know why I whispered, she can't hear me; I travel by thought. Probably it's because Mona is so knowledgeable. Being around her is similar to visiting a library. You don't presume to speak loudly in a library because of all the learning stored there.

I want to hear the proverbs and at least *one* of Mona's stories. But Kahu puts his hand on my back, saying, "We'll go to Kona and return when it's not raining."

"**I** hope it's not on raining on Maui," I say at the tree today.

"Fair weather," Kahu answers. Makahiki is winding down; I want you to see the last games and final ceremonies."

"No mango?"

"No need. He touches my back, and instantly we're on the field where I'ini won his spear-throwing and -sliding contests. Hundreds of people have formed a large circle around an open field. Something exciting must be about to begin.

Then it does: Five tattooed warriors, hair in topknots, wearing traditional loincloths, stride into the center of the field. Each of four has a wooden club; the other carries a shark-tooth dagger.

Five astonishing-looking women suddenly push through the crowd to stand facing the men. Bald, nude from the waist up, gleaming in the sun, they wear only a very short bark cloth *kapa* girdling their waists. Each carries a rolled-up rope with some sort of weight at one end.

I ask Kahu, "Who or what are those?"

"Female warriors trained in *lua:* Their hair was been pulled out so there is nothing for an opponent to grab, their bodies are oiled so they can't be gripped. The rope each holds is called a *pīkoi.* I think you are going to be *as-ton-ished,*" Kahu says, drawling it.

The men and women spread out. This will be one-on-one combat. What chance do these almost-naked ladies with little ropes have against burly brutes holding huge, deadly looking clubs? Standing close, I smell coconut oil on the women's heads and bodies and hear their deep, rhythmic breathing.

This will be a series of one-on-one demonstrations. *Ugh!* I think. The starter blows a conch shell and the gladiators begin.

Swish, swish! Women twirl their weighted device with their left hands. Are they doing a Persian whirling dervish dance? Poor things: The men, in attack positions, stomp forward, ready to strike. One raises his club for a deadly blow—planning to pulverize his opponent's slippery body as she calmly faces him, rhythmically swinging her cord. The biggest and bulkiest guy faces the largest woman warrior, holding his club in front of him with two hands. His legs are widespread as he stalks, ready to drive the club through his opponent's bare breasts. Aren't there any rules? This will be *ugly*.

Swish, swish, swish! Women calmly swing weighted ends, releasing more cord with each swirl.

It's over in an instant. A cord reaches the thighs of the man with the upraised club, binding his body and right arm. Another woman wraps the *pīkoi* around her opponent's neck and she's strangling him. Two women upend their foes, who've dropped their weapons. The largest lady ensnares her opponent's legs and drags him, flat on his back, off the field. She's a crowd favorite.

"They practice on tree stumps in their *lua* school and are excited to entangle men instead," says Kahu, grinning.

"**Y**ou watched priests collect gifts for Lono to start Makahiki. We'll go to the ocean to see the gifts being sent to him. That'll conclude Makahiki."

Travel is accomplished so easily with Kahu: One touch and I'm there. Men are tying a small canoe to a large double canoe. A chief, wearing a full-length feather cape and stately helmet, stands in the big canoe; sails flap behind him in the wind. Several warriors sit below, paddles in hand.

Kahu explains: "That single-hulled canoe is Lono's. The basket laced to its outrigger is filled with taro, sweet potatoes, bananas, and other foods. The king's canoe will pull Lono's canoe out to sea, then release it to its destination: Kahiki, ancestral home of Hawaiians.

"You mean 'Tahiti,' don't you?"

"'Kahiki' is the name in Hawaiian."

"Kahu, hardly any groceries are going to Lono in that small canoe."

"That's the system. This is a figurative finale. The *ali'i* standing up in the big canoe and his pals keep the gifts. They'll live off them until next year's ceremonies at each *ahupua'a*. Lono's gift boat is tied to the big boat that'll take to sea.

"We'll go now. There's no need to wait for the chief's return. Everything that happens is symbolic. I just wanted you to see for yourself what goes to Lono."

"You don't mean 'what goes,' you mean 'how little goes,'" I retort. "At least King Xerxes was open about his greed."

Ignoring my cynicism, Kahu continues: "A group of warriors will wait on shore for the high chief. When the *ali'i nui* and one of his warriors step out of their canoe, one of the warriors will run toward them, holding two spears. He'll throw one. The chief's man will easily ward it off. The attacker then goes up to the chief and touches him with the point of his second spear. He doesn't really harm him; the tip of his spear is covered with *kapa*. The purpose is to symbolize that the chief is impervious to harm—proof that he's a strong ruler.

"And worthy of all the largesse?"

"That, too.

"Lono's gifts have gone to sea. The *kapu* system is back in effect. The farming cycle begins. It is open season for wars again. Life in ancient Hawai'i resumes."

Kahu puts his arm over my shoulder and we return to Hospital Hill. There is a surprise at home: Josephine Hall, a public health nurse, will be sharing half of the house. I hadn't mentioned that our place is divided into two units.

28. Money Grows on Trees

It is early November 1942. Kahu, Per'fesser, and I sit near Menehune Plains in a little mountain cove surrounded by ferns. Per'fesser came to hang his finished "House of the Rising Sun" painting in Esther's queenly chamber. He says Aiko and Esther are talking about clothes.

"Some new material is coming to the Liberty House, and Aiko wants the queen to sketch some new designs. Actually, they will be ancient ones."

"How do you know that? My new neighbor Jo Hall says civilian goods shipping is very erratic because of German and Japanese submarines and that's why we have wartime shortages."

"Our information is from birds and fish," Per'fesser smiles smugly.

I must be looking surprised. Condescendingly, he explains: "Albatross soar over convoys, inform flying fish, who tell seagulls hanging around docks to watch for stevedores unloading Liberty House boxes.

"Gulls report this to mynah birds, who watch for unpackers at the department stores' loading dock. Mynah birds love to chatter, their news reaches dolphins playing in North Shore waters, and they tell porpoises who swim to Kaua'i. Young calves, loving to perform water tricks for Aiko, give her the glad news.

"She learned that Liberty House has new goods in stock and urged me to hurry over, hang my new painting, and put Esther in a designing mood! I have lots of cash for the store register; we'll be night shopping soon." He smiles. "We always pay."

Now changing the subject, Per'fesser becomes serious: "Kahu told me about what you've seen. You have reached the cusp. Ancient Hawai'i is about to change irrevocably."

Miki peeks from behind a tree fern. "Come out, Leprechaun!" Per'fesser calls. "We're about to discuss Hawai'i's emergence from the Stone Age."

Nodding his head docilely, Miki sits to my right, sighs, then recites:

> American trader Captain Metcalf
> Unwittingly provides cannons, muskets,
> And military advisors helping
> With strategies—battles unifying
> The Hawaiian Islands as one kingdom.
> Soon that system will fall like dominoes,
> One object falls against the next object,
> Causes it, in turn, to fall, and then that
> Causes another object to fall flat,
> 'Til nothing stands and it becomes
> 'The End.'

"Miki, we're moving forward and expanding Arthur's perspective."

He shakes his head sadly:

> Am very sad over the destruction
> Of trees with dryads beauteous in the breeze.
> Saving the environment makes more sense
> Than what happened to the *'iliahi.*

"That's a fine idea," Per'fesser replies. "Let's discuss *the environment.* Hawai'i has plants found nowhere else— silverswords on the painting I gave Queen Esther today, for instance.

He begins in didactic style: "Remember albatross symbolically hanging on the replica of Lono carried by priests to each *ahupua'a?* Albatross brought seeds that grew here."

My surprised look prompts Per'fesser to provide details. Before recording them in this journal, I acknowledge that sometimes I gulp my food, without chewing it carefully. *I do know* how digestive systems work. Birds or boys, they all gulp food.

This is what he explained: "Albatross, having an eleven-foot wingspan, soar over the Pacific from Hawai'i to Japan. They eat fish from the ocean—seeds, offal, and other things they find on land—dropping the outcome.

"Sandalwood is well established in southeastern Indonesia, Australia, as well as in India. Emu, Australia's six-foot-high birds, swallowed single-seeded sandalwood nuts—said to be quite delicious. Albatross scrounged for seeds in emu dung and deposited them on Hawai'i, where they grew profusely."

I ask, "Did other plants come the same way?"

"Indubitably," Per'fesser replies. "Albatross were Pacific planters."

He continues: "I speculate on the arrival of dryads, or hamadryads as sometimes called. These beautiful young women bond with trees they inhabit. Each lives as long as her bonded tree. Originally identified with oak trees, they diversified. In Hawai'i they chose *'iliahi*—sandalwood trees.

"Some may have been away vacationing when their trees were cut down and turned into masts—Balboa "discovered" the Pacific in 1513; Magellan explored it soon after.

"Let's surmise that these returning vacationers, feeling guilty about being away when their tree was felled, followed the masts. On the way they heard from albatross about *'iliahi* in Hawai'i. *'Iliahi* would be very appealing for a new bonding. Soon, every *'iliahi* in Hawai'i's lavish forests was connected with a dryad."

Queen Esther walks toward us, chanting:

> *Fair-haired dryads of the shady woods.*
> *Lips and limbs, and eyes and ringlets*
> *Swept by a spirit*
> *In the still enraptured air.*

Miki leans over and whispers:

> She speaks from Anderson's book, *The Dryads,*
> We know all about them in Ireland.

Esther continues, interpreting dryad existence:
"Dryads of the shady woods: All slim females about my size, just under or just over five feet high. All with pale

skin, hair generally red, a few being blonds. Pale-green eyes of young dryads aging into light brown.

"I loved what they wore—short, silky, translucent cloths tied around waist and breasts. Some leaving upper attributes bare.

"All sweet and good-natured—having only charming forest experiences. Rejoicing in the sunshine, shivering gleefully in the rain, talking with everything that could fly when they paid a visit, understanding the language of animals.

"Looking into clouds, they imagined thoughts of shapes forming there. All loved hearing of places I'd been. Before I left we joined hands, made a ring, and did some spinning.

"When mating, they placed in the ground an *'iliahi* seed from each of their bonded trees. It was braided together with a lock of their hair. Then they held each other in a dance, finishing with a long spin. They cut their left palms in a semicircular shape, one having it arch upward, the other downward. Placing both palms together, so cuts formed a circle, with fingers locked, they let their blood flow over the seed in the ground. Soon, a baby from both of them sprouted up into a tree, a dryad growing with it."

Esther ends abruptly: "I am leaving now, *don't want to hear the rest of your story.* You're providing Arthur with 'perspective.' He deserved to hear mine!" She gives me a stiff acknowledging nod.

Miki looks mournful as Esther stomps away. We remain quiet. After a bit, Per'fesser changes the mood: "Miki's verses referred to American sea captain Simon Metcalfe inadvertently setting forces in motion that led

Kamehameha I to destroying sandalwood trees on this island. His successors did so everywhere else. This initiated the domino affect felt by Kamehameha's successors until the independent kingdom ended.

"Kahu, let's take Arthur through some of the sequence. You describe events as a Hawaiian would, I'll present a white men's view. Then we'll take Arthur to see sandalwood trees and the beginning of decentralized Hawai'i's fall. Agreeable with you?"

Kahu nods, and Per'fesser begins.

"Simon Metcalfe, an American surveyor, acquired two ships and became a seal fur trader. He captained the brig *Eleanora* with his son Thomas accompanying him as captain of a small schooner called the *Fair American*. China was their market. The Metcalfes got into trouble with the Spanish navy for moving in on their sources for furs at Nootka Sound. The Spanish were almost at war with England over fur rights when the Americans appeared. Released from confinement at a Spanish naval base, the Metcalfes sailed to Hawai'i, picking up some seal skins from Eskimos before they left.

"Simon arrived first, at Kohala on this island. It was in 1789, ten years after Captain Cook was killed a few miles below us, at Kealakekua Bay. By then, a steady procession of ships was coming to Hawai'i. Natives viewed them as sources for competitive edges in battle. Nails and other pieces of metal they stole or traded from ships could be pounded into sharper, stronger weapons.

"Local chief Kame'eiamoku and some of his men came on board. Metcalfe didn't like their inquisitive behavior, suspecting they were snooping for metal. This American sea captain believed in strong and immediate punishment should his rules be broken. He resented the suspected pilferers' behavior and told his men to grab and tie the chief to the mast. *He would provide an example that these confounded natives would never forget!*

"Captain Metcalfe personally flogged Kame'eiamoku with a whip—the standard form of discipline on the high seas. It was much better than the next level: blindfolding a victim and forcing him to walk a plank leading from the boat—never knowing which next step would lead to drowning.

"Metcalfe insulted the chief's *mana,* violated all sorts of *kapu,* and disgraced Kame'eimoku in front of his subordinates. Kame'eiamoku vowed revenge on the ship carrying haole that came his way.

"Metcalfe's Hawai'i horror show had just begun. He sailed to Maui. There natives stole a small boat from the vessel and took a sleeping sailor with them. The story reached Metcalfe: 'The sailor, stationed in the boat to watch her, fell asleep while he rocked on the deep. *The natives murdered the poor fellow while he was on his knees supplicating for mercy. What depraved savages!'*

"This horror intensified Captain Metcalfe's rage. He sailed to Olowalu, the thieves' village, and learned his boat had been broken up for its nails—which stone-age men treasured as moderns do gems. The natives offered Metcalfe the sailor's bones—flesh had been scraped off in their respectful old-time fashion—as was done with Captain Cook.

"He screamed: *'Cannibalized!'* Neither he nor those serving under Cook understood Hawaiian burial customs.

"Cunningly, Metcalfe invited villagers to meet the ship, saying, 'I want to trade with you.' The canoes approached. *With a big aloha smile,* the American captain motioned for them to come to the other side. That was where his cannon was secured, loaded with ball and shot waiting for a spark. Metcalfe ordered an avenging broadside fired at point-blank range, blasting apart the canoes. This killed about a hundred Hawaiians and wounded several hundred more."

Kahu joins in: "Olowalu was considered a *puʻu honua,* a sanctuary and refuge, like the one at Hōnaunau. After the massacre, the Ugly American sailed to Kealakekua Bay, down below us."

Per'fesser continues: "Meanwhile, Thomas, Captain Metcalfe's son, has arrived near Kawaihae Bay in the *Fair American* schooner. This was Chief Kameʻeiamoku's territory. Humiliated by whip scars on his broad back, Kameʻeiamoku was eager for revenge. The *Fair American* was manned by four sailors and Thomas, the inexperienced nineteen-year-old captain. Angry Hawaiians captured it easily, killed Thomas, three of his crew, and injured Issac Davis, who for some reason Kameʻeiamoku spared.

"Kameʻeiamoku gave the ship, cannon, muskets, ammunition, goods, and Davis to Kamehameha.

"Captain Metcalfe sent John Young ashore to investigate; after blowing everyone up, he needed supplies for the rest of his journey. Kamehameha prohibited further contact with anyone from the *Eleanora*. Kealakekua was a ghost town. After waiting two days for Young to return, Metcalfe fired a cannon, hoping he'd hear it and it would guide him back. Frustrated, Captain Metcalfe left for China, unaware his young son had been killed.

"Kamehameha now had cannon, muskets, and two men experienced in the art of modern warfare. He gave them land, people to care for it, and royal Hawaiian women for wives. Young and Davis became Kamehameha's advisers and builders of his modern army.

"Metcalfe sailed to China with sea otter skins and some sandalwood acquired in Kealakekua Bay. This curiosity had a fragrant odor when burned. Chinese traders coming on board for furs told Metcalfe the wood was "gold."

"Some of Metcalfe's men spread this astonishing news through Macao's bars to other sailors, who told their captains—and this was the impetus for Hawai'i's gold rush.

"Americans from Boston persuaded Kamehameha to sign a monopoly agreement on the export of sandalwood that worked like this: Kamehameha would have sandalwood waiting for their ships, they would sail with it to Chinese ports, sell it, and give him one quarter of the net profits.

"It was an instant hit in China. The famous John Jacob Astor, a New York fur trader, financier, and America's richest man, predicted sandalwood would become the most valued item in the Hawaiian kingdom. He wanted in on it."

Kahu says, "Kamehameha controlled districts on this island where *'iliahi* grew profusely. Kamehameha didn't control all of the islands, but his fist covered most of Hawai'i. He lacked formal education but had a shrewd mind. He smelled a good thing and wanted absolute control over sandalwood trading. He told other chiefs they couldn't sell any without his approval—meaning without him being part of the action.

"He initially ordered men to go to the mountains and carry it to the landings. In spring, traders on the way to China with cargoes of furs came to Hawai'i to pick up sandalwood. The gold rush was on.

"Miki, come with us. We'll continue this story in the forests." He just shakes his head and walks dejectedly to the grotto.

Per'fesser says, "For the next episode, we must move ahead several years to the time when the sandalwood trade is well established and greed has infected these islands. Please transport Arthur, Kahu. See you there."

It is dawn, and we see thousands of commoners trudging up the slopes of valleys to toil in shadowed forests.

"They'll remain until sunset," Kahu explains. "Men hack down sandalwood trees, women and youngsters strip away branches. This is the way of life."

He points to a large pit gouged in the ground. "That is as long and as wide as a ship's hold. Workers have to fill it within a certain period of time, fulfilling sort of a production system."

People working in the forest are worn and emaciated— such a contrast to healthy, happy, well-fed people at Makahiki celebrations.

Kahu explains: "When the pit is filled, *maka'ainana* remove and drag logs down the hills to the beach, where they'll be dried and trimmed. When 'cured,' guide canoes float them to trading ships lying offshore."

Along treacherous mountain trails, families travel, logs and sandalwood strapped to shoulders. The forest is becoming a bare plain where dryads died.

Kahu takes me soaring over farmlands that now are wastelands. He explains, "People harvest *'iliahi* instead of farming. They have become sandalwood slaves. Famine is here. Greed grows instead.

"In time, Kamehameha will order more than six foreign ships, an arsenal of arms and ammunition, and storehouses of luxuries. He wants weapons to achieve his goals, but he is also highly vulnerable to gaudy trinkets and high-quality whiskey—Hawaiians have acquired a taste for it.

"Traders seize on his desire for supremacy by offering modern weapons and luxuries now for promissory notes that come due later."

"He will collect a storehouse of the white men's' long-distance fire weapons and fast ships. Traders tell the king, 'Order now and you can pay after your seasoned *'iliahi* is sold in China. You don't need cash flow for modern merchandise, you have sandalwood—just send logs to our ships.' Inadvertently, he and successors will mortgage the kingdom of Hawai'i to white traders. The system will become like "dominoes," as Miki described.

"This brave warrior is unaware of the law of diminishing returns, the perils of interest rates, how traders manipulate prices of what he purchases. He is no match for the business acumen of encroaching whites. His chief advisor, John Young, has but a third-grade education. Some pretty sharp business characters find their way to the Islands.

"Years after what we're witnessing, Kamehameha visits Kona and sees his people physically broken and starving. He puts his court followers to work and sets a personal example by toiling in Kona's taro and sweet potato patches. He says he will eat only what he grows.

Such a noble gesture. I don't know what he harvested. He never shared his wealth with the people."

Per'fesser interrupts: "I think he demonstrated *Hudibras*—Show Business— knowing that modern guns and ships were worth some of his ritualistic and inspirational stoop labor."

"You are being very haole, Per'fesser," Kahu says. "Hawaiians don't speak of *ali'i* in a negative way. Let's return to Menehune Plains."

I go home slightly confused after seeing lush farms turned into famine sites. Mother is out, and our nice new neighbor, Josephine Hall, knocks on the door, inviting me to dinner. Originally from Missouri, "Jo"—it's what I'm supposed to call her—is slightly older than Mother. She's a public health nurse, speaks directly, but you can tell she's at peace with herself. After dinner, she starts teaching me cribbage.

A few days later, Mother, Jo, and I go to the USO at Christ Church. Hospital Hill's mess men cooked "turkeys and the works," as they describe it. Everyone has a grand time. The "Boy from Syracuse" sings and Mrs. Hua and her hula group play guitar and ukulele and perform what is called "sit-down hula"—no wiggling hips because they're dancing on church property.

"Turkey trots" go home with each of us. "Birds," as they were described, left frozen from the mainland but defrosted during their boat ride to Hawai'i. Someone discovered it and refroze them—but they were already activated. Everyone left the USO with trots boiling in tummies.

For my first trip to McCandless Ranch the next day, I ride a mule to the slopes of Mauna Loa. My cowboy guide, Moses, says he's "a dwarf." He's about Kahu's size; since he's visible to anyone, he doesn't want the real world to know he's menehune. I don't let on what I know. Moses is sympathetic about many trot stops I need to make along the way.

Mauna Loa, the earth's largest volcano, is well over 13,000 feet above sea level. By mid-afternoon, fog covers the upper area where McCandless ranches. I ask my guide if he's ever seen *'iliahi* trees on the mountain.

"Yep, I know where one is, along with something else. We'll go tomorrow."

Is the something else a *dryad?* The next day, Gypsy, the mule I'm riding, follows Moses' horse through the dense fog until he calls back, "Over there." I get off the mule and look at the branches on a sandalwood tree—just like the ones I went to see being cut down.

Something huge is wrapped around the tree. Bug-eyed, I examine a U.S. Navy Grumman F4F-3 Wildcat fighter plane.

"It went off course in the fog and crashed here and we reported finding it," says cowboy Moses.

Can you imagine my excitement in examining a real fighter plane? Moses knows what I want.

"Take the .50 caliber machine gun with the twisted barrel. Leave the other. I don't think you'll get into trouble having a souvenir that won't fire."

I put it in my closet as Exhibit One for my wartime museum.

29. Stone Age Blasted Away

Ah Soong joins Miki, Kahu, and me under the eucalyptus tree; he brought *kūlolo*.

I tell him, "Kahu is going to describe Kamehameha's interest in a new kind of warfare invented in China."

Ah Soong smiles and says, "Oh yes, Chinese invent gunpowder during the ninth-century Song dynasty and use fireworks to scare away evil spirits."

He starts slicing the *kūlolo* with a knife carried under his smock.

"Go on," Kahu encourages him.

"In 1787, Kai'ana bring Kamehameha pistol and ammunition from Canton. Able to kill from a distance greater than a spear go is v-e-r-y interesting to Kamehameha. Two years later, Kame'eiamoku give cannon and muskets from the *Fair America* to Kamehameha. Young and Davis demonstrate it.

"Give the mighty cannon a Hawaiian name," Kamehameha orders.

"I will name it 'Lopaka,' after my father Robert," Mr. Young answered.

"Lopaka will help me conquer Maui," declared Kamehameha. I want you to train my men to use muskets."

Offering us pieces of coconut pudding, Ah Soong asks Kahu, "Will you show Arthur what happened?"

"Yes, but from a distance. Noisy Lopaka makes things gruesome. Want to come with us to Maui?"

"Oh my, yes," Ah Soong replies eagerly. "But hard for me to walk."

"We're flying. We'll see what happened about forty years before you and Ahung came from Macao to start a Maui sugar mill."

Within minutes, we four soar over green hills dropping to a rugged shoreline.

"This is Hana," Kahu explains, gliding on my right. "Ka'ulahea I, honored at the Makahiki for 'No warfare in his lifetime,' has a descendent who now is king of Maui. He's adopted his ancestor's name, and Ka'ulahea II is very quarrelsome. He has moved in on O'ahu, is extremely jealous of Kuali'i's and Pelei'oholani's reputation, and says their descendents 'are a doomed race.'"

"I don't like him," say I.

"Well, Kamehameha is here to give this disrespectful Maui upstart a life-ending lesson in modern warfare. Young and Davis will shoot Lopaka. They've taught many warriors to use muskets and have lots of ammunition.

"We are in the summer of 1790. Kamehameha must start and finish this war quickly before Makahiki halts it.

"Look down. The sea is almost black with canoes." Kahu provides details: "There are over 600 canoes holding 18,000 warriors from Kohala down there. That's the *Fair Haven* sailing in the front—first ship in what will become Kamehameha's modern navy.

"Kamehameha doesn't realize that Ka'ulahea II left for O'ahu and put his son Kalanikupule in charge.

"We'll soar over here, and I'll explain what's happening.

"Seeing this huge force causes Hana's people to surrender without a fight. Kamehameha accepts, instead of pillaging the village as a Celt army might—"

> Stop! It's unfair!
> Can't respond in the air!

Kahu smiles at the protesting leprechaun on our left. "Sorry, Miki, didn't mean to offend."

He continues: "Kamehameha explains he didn't come to loot, but is after the 'Ōlapu Adz, a sacred stone stolen from its shrine in Hilo. Hana people tell him a Maui chief in Makawao has it.

"'We'll send a runner to ask King Kalanikupule to send it back.'

"Informants advised this king that Kamehameha doesn't intend just to pick up the stone and sail away. They've seen Hawai'i warriors remove outriggers from the canoes, a sign that this massed army isn't just going to jump into their boats and return. 'They are after something more than a stone,' is what they say. 'Watch out for Kamehameha, he is very cunning.'"

Coming closer, Kahu motions: "We'll leave this Hana coast for another location."

Maui is varied and beautiful, particularly seen from fifty feet high. I watch the activity.

Kamehameha scatters his forces . . . sends a group of marchers along the Maui north shore . . . fleet members reattach outriggers . . . the flotilla heads westward, led by the *Fair American*.

Foot soldiers engage in one-on-one challenges. Outcomes of individual battles are pretty even. Kahu flies close to tell me Maui is known for outstanding warriors.

I can't tell who's winning. Uh-oh! Now I can.

The flotilla's in sight. Its sheer enormity causes Maui forces hurriedly to leave the combat area.

They retreat to a hill, and Kamehameha steps out from his ranks. You can't miss him, because he has a grand, long feather robe along with a feather helmet—but he's head and shoulders above everybody: Kahu says Kamehameha is seven feet tall!

He invites a Maui champion to come forward for one-on-one. Floating close, I hear his challenge, above the wind. I haven't had a mango, so I can't understand his shouting.

Kahu comes over and explains: "Kamehameha wants to settle the matter of who keeps the 'Ōlapu Adz. The chief who snitched it from Hilo has stepped forth."

He fights bravely, but not for long. Kamehameha kills him, but doesn't do anything messy like pulling out his heart or eating his eye. It is windy up here; I don't hear anything from my companions.

While Kamehameha is winning the adz, our vantage point reveals what wily Kalanikupule is doing.

Floating to my right, Kahu explains: "Knowing what previous sea invaders have done, the Maui king has split his forces to protect the leeward cost.

"This battle will last for a couple of days, so I'll summarize. You've seen lots of mobility from both armies, but Kamehameha plans to centralize his foes. We'll speed ahead in time for that outcome."

Now we're above 'Īao Valley, one of Hawai'i's most beautiful sights.

This monolith is known as "the Needle" for its singular sharp rise. It sits at the side of a steep-walled canyon with no exit to the mountains; a river runs at the base.

Kahu gestures to come near and hear him. Moving in the air is effortless: I give a flutter kick and I'm at his side as we glide into the valley. He explains: "Maui forces moved into this stronghold to make a stand. There were five reasons why this is an ideal base to hang out for a long siege: One, steep inclines make it impenetrable to mass assault; two, by spear thrusts defenders can pick off aggressors, one-by-one, seeking to climb the sharp inclines; three, the valley has a clean, clear stream of water; four, this is a planting area, terraced with taro patches, surrounded by mud dikes containing ample food supply of everything Hawaiians grow to eat, as well as medicinal plants—it is easily defended; five, food is easily accessible to those in the upper valley. Defenders can sit up there and eat well, picking off foe below one by one, until the starving enemy below leaves.

"But cunning Kamehameha has turned the traditional advantage of defending this location into a disadvantage. Watch what is approaching. Very shortly, he will blast

Hawai'i out of the Stone Age. This is the third day of the Maui battle. It is the last day of olden times."

Kamehameha's army has pushed the Maui forces into 'Iao Valley and directed 1,200 of his warriors to cover the front of the valley. Here come the two haole advisers and warriors pulling Lopaka on a wheeled cart. Kamehameha's sandalwood trading has resulted in Wellington's grand British Army uniforms for Lopaka's cannon firers. Davis and Young certainly are stylish. A good number of Hawaiians follow carrying muskets on their shoulders; they've learned the British regimen.

Miki paraphrases lines of the fate facing Maui warriors. That battle, a cavalry charge described by Alfred Lord Tennyson, will occur almost sixty-five years after this one:

> In the valley of death . . .
> Cannon in front of them
> Volleyed and thundered.

Ah Soong claims to enjoy fireworks but leaves once the red-mouthed cannon starts blasting.

Maui warriors in the back row, trying to climb the cliffs, seem out of range of the musket shooters. Lopaka booms at massed bodies everywhere, and they fall into the stream. Maybe I am imagining, but a young man crawling on the other side of the cliff resembles I'ini. I just have a glimpse before he disappears from sight—he may have escaped the slaughter.

Kahu motions: "No more, let's return to Kona."

I look down on a red river: Clogged with bodies, it is overflowing. Maui women along the hillside are wailing. This reminds me of a song Mr. Hua sings:

Malu . . . Malu i ke ao . . .
Kea hi o Wailuku . . .
Kepaniwai aʻo ʻĪao.

"Kepaniwai aʻo ʻĪao" means "the dammed waters of ʻĪao," Kahu says softly.

"You saw the first of Hawaiʻi's two most horrible massacres, both caused by modern weaponry," Kahu says when we all collect at Menehune Plains.

"Ten years later, with more and bigger cannons and many guns, Kamehameha repeats today's tactics. He drives Oʻahu's army to the Pali, pushes them to the cliffs, and from there they drop to death.

"There were no battles after the one on the Pali. Kamehameha rules supreme over the Hawaiian Islands, amasses his sandalwood riches, shows his friend, the English Captain Vancouver, the flag he's designed. It resembles England's "Union Jack" flag. British start describing Kamehameha as the *Emperor of the Pacific*.

"Today you glimpsed ancient Hawaiʻi coming to an end."

30. Queen Esther's Revenge

"Joy to the World" is among songs we sing during the Miller's Christmas party. Margaret, the Miller's blond, pigtailed daughter, is home for the holidays from Punahou School on Oʻahu. Her father loves poetry, so for a Christmas gift Margaret memorized Henry Wadsworth Longfellow's *Paul Revere's Ride*. As she recites it for us, Poppa looks so very proud. How was she able to memorize all of that and through her voice transport us to New England where it happened—and make it possible for us to feel as though we were on a galloping horse?

As my contribution, I played Antonin Dvorak's *Humoresque* as a violin solo. The title is a German word for mood, state of mind. It's both peppy and sentimental, matching the holiday mood.

Living in several worlds fosters views I can't share—especially when people tell holiday stories. That's why this journal is a *catharsis*—I used that new word with Dr.

Mendelsson. She asked, "In what context do you apply this?

"In considering my thoughts."

"When you're older, you should read about Carl Gustav Jung's boyhood."

One of mother's clients gave us a duck. We've tied a string to its foot and attached the string to a stake in our backyard. I feed it and am supposed to prepare it so mother can roast it for my birthday dinner, five days after Christmas.

I haven't seen menehune since traveling to ʻĪao. Mother went to Oʻahu for a meeting, and Jo Hall has been cooking dinner for me. It is time to return the favor. I tell her, "I'm going to prepare pancakes for dinner and will fry Portuguese sausage."

Being a host is a big responsibility; maybe that's why my stomach has felt strange all day. Coming to watch me flip flapjacks, Jo Hall says, "You're acting disoriented and your face is flushed."

"Just excited," I reply.

She sticks a thermometer in my mouth, reads it, and acts alarmed. Immediately she drives me to Kona Hospital. All I can remember from that point on is dizziness, being dressed in a short green gown, given some shots, and having an ether mask placed over my face.

I wake up in a hospital bed. A nurse tells me, "The doctor removed your appendix. Here it is floating in this little bedside jar, a souvenir for you. It burst. We're treating you for peritonitis; you'll be here for a while."

Don't remember much more than that until two visitors pop in. I show them the little jar.

"Ugh," Kahu says. "A broken baby eel."

Miki sees something different:

> You had a small snake: those St. Patrick chased
> Away from Ireland in such great haste.

Kahu seems excited as he explains, "We came to tell you about what Queen Esther did because Kamehameha cut down the *'iliahi*."

"I want to hear this. Help me prop up this pillow so I can look down on you from this hospital bed."

Kahu starts the story; Miki's eyes twinkle.

"Esther had been brooding in your cave ever since we took you to see *'iliahi*. Orienting on the *'iliahi* forests reawakened some of her angst. She decided to travel back to 1819, after Kamehameha was dead, when the kingdom was being run jointly by his twenty-two-year-old son Liholiho and by his favorite wife Ka'ahumanu.

"Kamehameha had twenty-two wives, but Ka'ahumanu was his best pal. Big, smart, with a good brain, she was the only person who, in private, dared tell him what to do—and he'd do it!

"Liholiho already had five wives; his favorite was his sister. This young man liked to drink—maybe acquiring the taste from his dad. Kamehameha had known Liholiho didn't have what it would take to rule the kingdom, so he appointed Ka'ahumanu as a co-ruler.

"You learned about the restrictive *kapu* system and how especially hard it was on women.

"Esther decided to take revenge on Kamehameha. While Ka'ahumanu slept, our fairy queen whispered ideas into her ears: 'Why should only men have the tastiest foods? Who says gods will strike down anyone violating a *kapu?* Do gods really tell priests to do violent things, or is it in their *kahuna's* nature? Men aren't superior, they just have more opportunities. The gods are just hunks of wood without power. It is the priests who exert authority, in behalf of gods, and who demand death.

"'What would happen if you, our supreme queen, stood up for *all women?* Liholiho will do what he's told. Invite him to dinner, then abolish all *kapu*. Knock down those hunks of wood that *kahuna* say are gods. Women deserve equality! You have the authority to make it happen.'

"I don't know what else Esther breathed in Ka'ahumanu's ears; she is very persuasive, as you know."

Jumping up and down impatiently, Miki warns:

> Hurry up Kahu and go to the end,
> I hear the night nurse coming round the bend.
> She'll think Arthur's flipped, talking to himself
> Instead of learning history from an elf.

Kahu hurriedly wraps things up: "Ka'ahumanu thinks she dreamed those ideas during a good night's sleep. The next evening, she invites Liholiho to dinner. He comes; ladies are waiting on them. Enjoying lots of good whiskey, he becomes mellow, and all his favorite foods are served. Ka'ahumanu carries on a charming conversation *while eating the same things!*

"She compliments him on being progressive. 'How nice to dine together.' Then she explains what 'they' must do.

"He does it. The next day King Liholiho declares that the *kapu* system is over and orders *heiau* to be closed. He orders his troops to topple over the gods and to shut up protesting *kahuna*. There's a small-scale revolt against him on Hawai'i; Liholiho's army quickly squelches it. They have cannons and muskets!"

"Queen Esther is beaming. Liholiho, Kamehameha the Second, changes Hawai'i forever. We'll show you the outcome when you are recovered.

"Have to go—I hear the nurse's keys jingling. Err . . . you're not going to take that 'thing in the jar' home, are you?"

I shake my head. It's only a hospital curiosity.

Miki has to be the last heard. Before they head out the door he winks and says:

> Always make certain a woman's your friend,
> Otherwise she will get you in the end.

He giggles and disappears.

Epilogue

A few days later, Uncle Bob visits me in the hospital. We're enjoying the duck dinner Mother had him bring. He's wearing a white sailor suit, looks terrific, and says, "I'm training on Maui and was allowed a few days off to come see how you're doing."

"I'm healing fine, have been receiving shots of a wonder drug called penicillin, and will be going home soon. What can you tell me?"

"Being a submariner who is an Island boy, they've turned me into 'A Naked Swimmer.'"

"Really naked?"

"No, we wear swimming shorts instead of diving gear. It's a new concept. At the university I studied reefs and beaches, and the navy thinks I might have some knowledge of atolls and islands. We go south, leave our sub and swim around observing water currents, sandbars, and checking out beaches. This is surveillance, preparation before our fighting men make beach landings. We come back to Pearl Harbor and prepare charts. America is going to win this war! That's all I can tell you."

"You can tell me something more. Why does Grandpa resent being Hawaiian? Why do I have to hide what I am learning?"

"You can pass for haole," Bob answers.

He put his partially finished duck dinner on my tray table.

"This is a sad story. I'll give you highlights—maybe you'll learn more later. Your mother and Sam tell me you are becoming a genealogist."

I've finished the crackling skin and start chewing on a duck leg as Uncle Bob tells his story.

"Grandpa was a Big Island cowboy who enjoyed a fine horse, strong, sturdy dogs, a cattle drive or roundup, and other creations of Nature. Very smart, he is basically self-educated; he went to work to help bring up his sixteen brothers and sisters.

"He was smart enough to become principal of Makapala School in Kohala and be a Salvationist at nights. Belden has told you about the problems he had about seeing a white woman, your grandmother, when he first joined the Salvation Army.

"Dad always wanted to accomplish something significant for Hawaiians, just as his grandparents did by starting Hilo Boarding School. He told Aunt Emma Lyman Wilcox of his aspirations—she was the youngest child of the second-generation of missionary Lymans. The Wilcox family invested in turning the nineteenth-century Lyman house into a museum. Dad said he had a twentieth-century outgrowth of the Hilo Boarding School in mind. The Wilcox family helped him realize his dream by funding the Salvation Army Boys Home in Kaimukī.

"With community coworkers and friends, he turned a red desert and dusty slope into a pleasant haven for youth. They cleared land, added buildings for classrooms and dormitories, and started a school and farm. All of this required hard work, initiative, courage, and hope, while he had a hundred maladjusted boys to control.

"His landmarks stand in roads, stone walls, trees, lawns, and the modeling of many youths who showed themselves capable of living normal lives in this complicated world.

"Grandpa gave talks in public. Thinking you were going to ask about him, I brought a copy of one he gave before a United Welfare organization. He was a powerful speaker who attracted a great deal of attention in London serving directly under General Booth."

I read his brief speech entitled "Half Acre Per Boy":

I saw the impossible boy made the responsible boy and proud of it. I saw boys, who once wouldn't stay in school, itching to get into their gardens and to study their livestock.

I saw the chronic runaway become a good gym team leader. I saw nervous, shifty-eyed, underfed youngsters develop into responsible citizens. I saw all of this multiplied in dozens of cases.

They thrive from plenty of fresh air, lots of open space, good plain food, a clean bed, and occasionally some medical care. All that, with a little fatherly guidance, is the opportunity offered needy boys of this community by the Salvation Army Boys' Home.

"Attention he received in Honolulu proved his downfall.

"After enthusiastic response to his speech at the Honolulu Rotary Club, Dad told his commander, 'I'd like to become associated with such a fine organization.'

"'Rotary is not for people like you,' he answered.

"There were those who thought this Hawaiian man had to be put down. He was pushed into early retirement.

"He was a good man of the wrong color. That became his psychological handicap. We who loved him realized it.

"He is haunted by ghosts of racial inferiority."

I ask Uncle Bob, "When did all of this happen?"

"He was shown the door while you were in California."

(End)